And a little child shall lead them.
—*Isaiah* 11:6

For "Parkers" everywhere

Acknowledgments

Grateful to the very talented folks who help me
make my books everything they can be:
Melissa Endlich and the dedicated staff
at Love Inspired.

More thanks to the gang at Seekerville
(seekerville.net), a great place to hang out
with readers—and writers.

I've been blessed with a wonderful network
of supportive, encouraging family and friends.
You inspire me every day!

"Erin Kinley?"

Her slender frame stiffened, and she slowly spun to face him. Wearing an expression that Cam suspected mirrored his own, she rolled her hazel eyes toward the sky. "Now I know why Natalie didn't mention the owner's name."

"And why she didn't tell me who was interested. She must've figured neither of us would ever agree to do this if we knew who we were meeting."

"She's a smart girl." Glancing around, she folded her arms in an unhappy gesture he remembered all too well. "I haven't seen you since Drew and Bekah's wedding. How have you been?"

Still a little porcupine with Southern-lady manners, he noted with a grin. It was nice to know some things in his hometown hadn't changed. "Fine. And you?"

"Fine."

They stared at each other for a few seconds, and he was struck by the realization that she was a lot prettier than the persistent tagalong he and Drew had spent so much time ditching when they were all growing up together.

Mia Ross loves great stories. She enjoys reading about fascinating people, long-ago times and exotic places. But only for a little while, because her reality is pretty sweet. Married to her college sweetheart, she's the proud mom of two amazing kids, whose schedules keep her hopping. Busy as she is, she can't imagine trading her life for anyone else's—and she has a pretty good imagination. You can visit her online at miaross.com.

Books by Mia Ross

Love Inspired

Oaks Crossing

Her Small-Town Cowboy
Rescued by the Farmer
Hometown Holiday Reunion

Barrett's Mill

Blue Ridge Reunion
Sugar Plum Season
Finding His Way Home
Loving the Country Boy

Holiday Harbor

Rocky Coast Romance
Jingle Bell Romance
Seaside Romance

Hometown Family
Circle of Family
A Gift of Family

Visit the Author Profile page
at Harlequin.com for more titles.

Hometown Holiday Reunion

Mia Ross

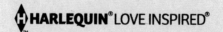

Recycling programs for this product may not exist in your area.

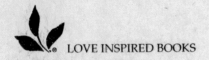 LOVE INSPIRED BOOKS

ISBN-13: 978-0-373-81939-3

Hometown Holiday Reunion

www.Harlequin.com

Printed in U.S.A.

Chapter One

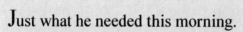

Just what he needed this morning.

Cam Stewart stood in the middle of the bustling kitchen at the Oaks Café, glowering at the commercial fridge that was making an ominous thunking noise. It had started last week, just after Christmas, as more of a loud hum punctuated by a bang every now and then. Now it was clanking with a fairly constant rhythm, and even though he wasn't an expert on large appliances, as a construction foreman he'd been around enough faltering equipment to recognize a death knell when he heard one.

Glancing over at the dishwasher who'd come running to get him, Cam shrugged. "That's how you know it's Monday, right?"

Until that moment, Kyle had looked terrified, as if he feared that his job was in danger because he'd been the one to deliver bad news.

The poor kid's tight expression loosened up, and he nodded. "I guess so."

In all honesty, Cam wasn't surprised by this latest in a seemingly endless parade of troubles. When he'd returned to Oaks Crossing in the fall to help out with the family business, he'd found the books and the property in a shambles, on the brink of failing altogether. His plans for sticking around for just a few weeks to rehab the building for sale had gone on an indefinite hold. No matter how good the shell looked, no one in their right mind would buy a restaurant that was on the verge of bankruptcy.

Putting that gloomy thought out of his mind, he focused on what he could control. "All right, Kyle, let's shut down this beast before something completely lets go in there. I'll call over to the appliance repair shop and see if they can send someone out today. For now, let's shift everything into the fridge over in the snack bar." A scary thought occurred to him, and he said, "Please tell me the walk-in freezer is still working."

"Last time I checked it was okay."

The hedging answer made Cam laugh, mostly because as much as he wanted to throw a fit, that wouldn't get any of their equipment fixed. That, and he was just too tired from a long string of sixteen-hour days to summon the energy. "Let's hope it stays that way. Grab one of the busboys to give you a hand."

"You got it, boss."

Clearly relieved that someone had arrived with a plan to save the day, Kyle hurried out front to find another set of hands that weren't already occupied clearing breakfast dishes from the tables. Cam was thumbing through the contact list on his phone when it started ringing in his hand. After checking the caller ID, he answered the call. "Hey, Nat. How's my favorite little sister?"

"Busy as a one-armed paper hanger. You?"

It had been one of their late grandfather's trademark sayings, and hearing it from her made Cam smile. "Same. I thought Realtors kept their own hours. What's got you up at the crack of dawn?"

"I've got a hot lead for the building next to the café."

Her tone alerted him that there was more to the story, and he got a firm grip on his temper before saying, "I hear a *but* in there."

"They'd like to rent it for a few months to make sure it's going to work for them."

Which meant he'd be stuck in his backwater hometown, playing nice with a tenant he didn't want in an attempt to keep them happy—and on the hook to purchase it. In the end they might not even buy the building, and he'd be right back where he started. "Not a chance."

"I knew you'd say that, but listen to me. Even though Kentucky winters are nothing compared to what you get up in Minnesota, this is a horrible time of year to sell property. After the holidays, no one wants to even think about laying out money like that. When spring arrives in a few months things might get better—but with the economy around here the way it is, you never know."

"You mean I might have to wait until spring to get rid of it?" Cam felt a frustrated growl threatening in the back of his throat, and he swallowed to keep it in check. "I have a life to get back to in Minneapolis, y'know. My boss has been real understanding, but once building season starts, he'll have to hire a new foreman to run the crew."

"That's why I called. At least with a tenant, you'd have some money coming in. Right now, you're stuck paying utilities and taxes on that place, with no income to offset the expense."

Despite the fact that she was telling him something he definitely didn't want to hear, Cam couldn't help feeling proud of his younger sister. He'd contributed a fair chunk of her college fund himself, and it was gratifying to see firsthand that she was making the most of her education. With a solid career, a doting husband and an adorable baby named Sophie, Natalie had what everyone wanted.

Sounded like a dream life for anyone. Except for Cam, of course.

His ill-fated marriage had been more than enough to sour him on the conventional lifestyle so many of his friends had fallen into. No attachments, no regrets, he'd vowed, even before the ink on his divorce papers had dried. The closer someone got, the easier it was for them to destroy you. Since he wasn't a masochist, he wasn't keen on going through that ever again.

The past was done and gone, so he brushed it aside and got back to the problem at hand. He hated the idea of being a landlord, but considering the fact that there currently weren't any other options visible on the horizon, he didn't seem to have a choice. "I guess I should at least meet your clients. When are they coming?"

"I said you'd meet them there in five minutes."

"Thanks for the heads-up, sis."

"I know you. If I'd given you more time, you'd have come up with a hundred reasons not to go," she shot back in a businesslike tone that made him grind his teeth. "This way, it'll be over soon and you can get on with your day."

It wasn't her fault that his week had started out so badly, Cam reminded himself. So, in the interests of family harmony, he swallowed his frustration and tried to sound appropriately grateful. "You've got a point there. Thanks for the lead."

"Anytime. When you're finished, give me a call to let me know how it went."

"Will do."

Hanging up, Cam checked in the kitchen and was pleased to find that nothing else had gone wrong. His call to the appliance repair shop was picked up by voice mail, so he left a message. Stopping in the cramped office to get a set of keys, he had the nagging feeling that he'd soon be hunting around for a decent used cooler. There was no way he could afford a new one.

The misty late-December air was cool, but nothing like he'd gotten used to during his ten years up north. On mornings like this, he really missed being part of a crew that built things instead of running around putting out fires that never seemed to end. Sure, he'd worked like a dog up in Minnesota, but at the end of the day, he'd accomplished something and went home feeling good about what he'd done.

Unfortunately, now he never got away from

his family's restaurant. It was a real stretch for someone accustomed to looking out for himself, and the responsibility weighed heavily on him. Miserable as he was, though, he just couldn't bring himself to leave his mother and sister to manage everything on their own. Whether it took another week or several months, he was committed to staying until he felt confident they'd be all right. But some days, he honestly worried that if he couldn't square things and leave soon, they'd be hauling him out of town in a straitjacket.

That pessimistic thought had just left his head when he turned the corner and discovered who was waiting for him on the sidewalk in front of the For Sale sign.

"Erin Kinley?"

Her slender frame stiffened, and she slowly spun to face him. Wearing an expression that he suspected mirrored his own, she rolled her hazel eyes toward the sky. When they came back to him, they weren't exactly friendly. "Now I know why Natalie didn't mention the owner's name."

"And why she didn't tell me who was interested. She must've figured neither of us would ever agree to do this if we knew who we were meeting."

"Smart girl." Glancing around, Erin folded

her arms in an unhappy gesture he remembered all too well. "I haven't seen you since Drew and Bekah's wedding. How have you been?"

Still a little porcupine with Southern-lady manners, he noted with a grin. It was nice to know some things in his hometown hadn't changed. These days, he doubted that even the most compassionate person in town wanted to hear what was actually going on with him, so he fell back on an old standby. "Fine. And you?"

"Fine."

They stared at each other for a few seconds, and he was struck by the realization that she was a lot prettier than the persistent tagalong he and Drew had spent so much time ditching when they were all growing up together. Her light brown hair was pulled back into a wavy ponytail, framing a pixie face still lightly freckled from the summer.

And then there were those eyes. A unique combination of green and gold, he knew they could twinkle with humor one second and slice through you the next. Smart and sassy, the Kinley boys' only sister had ridden roughshod over them all their lives. And for some reason Cam had never been able to fathom, every one of them just stood by and let her do it.

Realizing the silence had dragged on for a while, he kick-started their lagging discussion by dangling the keys. "Still wanna see inside?"

"Sure," she replied, lifting a shoulder as if it didn't matter much one way or the other.

But something in her expression said otherwise, and Cam got the feeling that renting this vacant building was just as important to her as it was to him. The idea that she might be in some kind of trouble entered his mind, but he pushed it aside as he strolled over to unlock the glass-paneled door. Her personal life was absolutely none of his business, he reminded himself sternly. If things worked out, they'd be professional neighbors, and his only concern would be whether or not her rent checks cleared.

With the mess his life was in right now, he didn't have the time—or the strength—to take on anyone else's problems.

He opened the door and stepped back to let her walk through ahead of him. The air was a little musty, but opening the windows would take care of that. Not wanting to get in her way, he stayed near the front and let her wander around the large, empty space, curious to hear what she thought.

One thing about Erin, he mused, you never had to worry about her sugarcoating her opinions to avoid hurting your feelings. Good or bad, she always told it like it was.

"Obviously," she started off in a brisk, no-nonsense manner, "I can't run a retail business in this canyon of a room. I'll need display cases and shelving, both on the floor and hung from the walls, which need to be painted something other than this lovely beige. Do you want to lay down some ground rules for what I can and can't do?"

He wasn't crazy about having to rip out a lot of furnishings if she ultimately decided not to take this albatross off his hands. Then again, if he let her do pretty much what she wanted, it might entice her to sign the purchase agreement sooner rather than later. While he meant to sound agreeable, he was stunned to hear himself saying, "Not really. If you want, I'll even build the stuff for you."

Her eyes widened in surprise. "Seriously?"

"Sure." It wasn't like him to leap out there like that, and he was already regretting the impulsive offer. But he'd done it, and there was no backpedaling from it now. "Now that the renovations on the café are finished, I've got some spare time. And spare lumber," he added, hoping to sweeten the deal.

"Thanks. I'll keep that in mind." Flashing him a grateful smile, she continued her assessing stroll. "This building's been vacant for a while now. When were the furnace and water heater last serviced?"

"I had 'em done about a month ago, when I repaired the roof. I did that myself, but mechanicals aren't my specialty so an HVAC company from Ferndale took care of those. You can call them if you want."

Her icy demeanor thawed slightly, and she gave him a tiny smile. "That's not necessary. I believe you."

"Because I'm Drew's friend?" He cringed at the insecurity he heard in his voice, and he covered it with a grin, hoping she'd assume he'd been joking.

"Because in spite of our *many* differences, you're a good guy and I know you wouldn't lie about something that important to trick me into leasing this place." She paused with a somber look, as if she was trying to decide if she should continue. After a few moments, she went on, "The main reason I'm asking is that my son and I will be living in the apartment upstairs. I want to make sure he's comfortable and safe."

Son? Cam was no actor, and he couldn't have disguised his astonishment if he'd wanted to. "I had no idea you were a mom."

"The ring bearer at Drew and Bekah's wedding was my foster son, Parker Smith."

The name and circumstances rang a bell in his memory, and for some reason he felt a rush of relief. Close on its heels came the thought that this tenacious, protective woman would probably make a fantastic mom. Shoving that observation aside, he said, "Oh, right. I think Drew mentioned that, but I didn't know the details."

"Parker's had a really tough time of it," she confided softly, looking up at the ceiling, then around the dusty interior, before coming back to Cam. "I can't change what happened to him in the past, but I'm determined to make sure he has a better future."

"It sounds like you're thinking about adopting him."

"I am, but Social Services has to try locating his parents first. All he could tell them was he was born in Kentucky and that he and his mother lived in a lot of different places."

"With such a common last name, it'd be almost impossible to find the right family, even if you had some idea where to look."

"Very true," Erin agreed with a resigned sigh. "Anyway, I'll be filing the paperwork ten minutes after his parents are officially declared unreachable."

He admired her generosity in taking on someone else's child and raising him on her own. "You haven't changed a bit. I lost track of how many critters you rescued when we were kids."

"There were a few," she acknowledged with a smile. "Mom and Dad used to pretend they didn't notice me sneaking them up to my room. It gave me time to come up with a good reason to keep them until they were better. Just before Dad died, I started the Oaks Crossing Rescue Center out at the farm. The day we opened, he said he'd never been prouder of me."

Her wistful tone made Cam frown. "I'm sorry you all lost him. Justin was a great man, and I really admired him. He stepped up bigtime when my dad left, and I'll never forget how hard he tried to help me."

"He thought you had a lot of potential."

"Too bad I proved him wrong."

"Oh, please," she scoffed, clearly trying to switch tracks to something slightly more cheerful. "You could've done anything you wanted, but we all know you chose construction 'cause it would give you the best tan."

Her accusation made him laugh, something he hadn't done much of the past few months. "Got me there."

Shaking her head, she looked past him to the door that led upstairs. "Is it liveable up there?"

"I guess that depends on how picky you are."

"What's that supposed to mean?"

"Don't get all riled up, bug," he said, making a calming gesture with his hands. "It's just that I remember you being pretty fussy about things like that. Now that you're a mom, I figure you must be even more worried about it."

"*Do not* call me that," she spat, just about tearing the old door off its hinges. "We're not kids anymore."

Tell me about it, Cam mused as he followed her up the creaky wooden steps. Two years younger than he was, the very headstrong Erin Kinley had always been a handful. Now she was even more so, and he pitied the guy who was unfortunate enough to lose his head over her.

She'd probably hand it back to him on a platter.

In truth, Erin didn't need a tour of the building to know she wanted it.

What she did need, however, was a few minutes to get over her shock at finding out that Cam Stewart was the owner. It made sense, she supposed, since the closed shop was right next to the diner and attached Laundromat he'd been running since coming home a few months ago. The reason for that was well-known around town, and she felt guilty for not asking about it sooner. "So, how's your mom doing?"

"Depends on the day," he replied with a frown. "Recovering from a stroke can be like that, from what the visiting nurse says. Sometimes Mom seems like she's getting back to her old self, and other times I can tell she doesn't quite recognize me when I get there."

Erin couldn't imagine how that would feel, and despite the fact that they'd never gotten along, her heart went out to him. "That's awful, Cam. I'm so sorry."

"It is what it is."

He shrugged, but the careless gesture wasn't nearly enough to mask the pain that made his brown eyes look almost black. The shadows under them told her that he'd been working way too hard and worrying more than anyone should have to. He still kept his dark, wavy hair a bit too long for her taste, but she couldn't deny that the years he'd spent up north had been good to him. More weathered than handsome, his features were an interesting combination of angles and creases that hinted at a lot of laughter.

Not recently, though, she realized sadly. Her

own life had gotten pretty complicated since her father's sudden death a few years ago, so she could relate. Thankfully, a much brighter topic popped into her head. "I just remembered you're a new uncle. How did Sophie like her first Christmas?"

"About like you'd expect," he responded with a chuckle. "I hunted all over for the baby doll Natalie said she'd like best, and what does my scamp of a niece do? She rips off the paper, chucks the toy away and plays with the box."

He fished out his cell phone and opened his pictures to show Erin a photo of a laughing little girl wearing a red velvet dress, one black patent shoe and reindeer antlers.

"Oh, she's adorable. How old is she now?"

"Ten months," he responded, glancing at the photo before sliding his phone back into his pocket. "The way she's moving around, she'll be walking any day. Then her parents will really have their hands full."

"If Sophie's anywhere near as popular as her mother was in high school, Alex will be busy intimidating all her possible boyfriends." Pausing, Erin gave Cam a stern look. "Maybe you can give him some lessons on that."

"I never wasted time intimidating anyone. I flat-out told 'em that if they got outta line with my little sister, I'd make 'em sorrier than they'd ever been in their miserable lives."

"My mistake. You threatened them."

"Got that right." He punctuated his response with a growl that would have been more convincing if his eyes hadn't been twinkling in fun. "Don't give me that look. All three of your brothers did the same thing for you."

Shaking her head in exasperation, Erin shared her opinion on that. "You were a bunch of morons, all four of you."

"Maybe, but we got our point across." When she didn't say anything, he flashed her a shameless grin. "You're welcome."

She couldn't come up with a witty comeback for that one, so she let the subject drop and strolled around the apartment, assessing what kind of home it would make for Parker and her.

While it wasn't large, it had a nice-sized living room with a bay window that overlooked Main Street. Both bedrooms were down a short hallway, on either side of a bathroom that would benefit from a good scrubbing but was otherwise acceptable. She wasn't much of a cook, but the galley kitchen and its appliances were in decent condition, and the breakfast bar separating it from the living area would do double duty for eating and homework.

"So," he began in a conversational tone, "I

can't help wondering why a lifelong country girl like you is suddenly interested in moving to town."

"I've been renting the bottom half of the old Johnson place for the past couple of years, but they've been hinting at selling it so they can move to Ohio to be closer to their grandkids. When Judge Markham decided to retire in December, he gave me a nice severance and a glowing reference about the administrative work I did for him. It was a decent job, but not really my thing. I mostly stayed because he and Granddad were friends for so long, and I could work flexible hours when I needed to."

"Because you're a mom now," Cam filled in with an incredulous look. "I'm still trying to wrap my head around that one."

So was she, Erin had to admit. But only to herself. She feared that if she ever voiced the tiniest smidgen of self-doubt, it would somehow get back to Parker's social worker and she'd lose him to the system she was so determined to rescue him from.

Eight years old, he was on the verge of being considered unadoptable, which meant a forever home was almost out of reach for the shy boy. Over the past few months, she'd made slow but steady progress with him, until he now looked her in the eye without flinching. She hated to consider what might happen to him if he was torn from the life she and her large, loving family had worked so hard to give him.

So, in typical Kinley fashion, she'd simply decided that she wasn't going to let that happen. "Anyway, I've been thinking about starting my own business, and with the apartment up here, this place would be perfect."

"For what?"

He seemed genuinely interested, and her heart leaped with the excitement she always felt when she talked about the dream that had edged closer to reality over the past year. "A pet store. Not your average one, though."

"Of course not," he said with a chuckle. "You never do anything like anyone else."

There was a tinge of admiration in his tone, and she couldn't keep back a smile. "You make that sound like a good thing."

"It is. There's plenty of boring, predictable folks on the planet. We certainly don't need any more." Leaning against the counter that divided the kitchen from the living room, he said, "What've you got in mind?"

"All right," she shot back, eyes narrowing suspiciously. "Who are you, and what have you done with Cam Stewart?"

"Whaddya mean?"

"You're being nice to me."

"I'm nice." When she gave him a wilting look, he laughed. "Okay, maybe that's a stretch. But I can be pleasant, if the situation warrants it."

"Meaning this one does?" He nodded, and after studying his serious expression she opted to give him the benefit of the doubt. After all, it wasn't like he could still stuff her in a locker and stand outside of it laughing his head off while she tried to bang her way free. "Well, I was planning on stocking all the usual supplies, but also some fancier things for people who like to spoil their animals. I'm going to call it Pampered Pets."

"I like it. Pretty much sums up what you're offering to your customers."

"Kind of like the new Wash and Dine Snack Bar you opened next to the café," she commented, figuring it was only fair to compliment him in return. "We've needed a Laundromat for a while, but you went one further and made it into a fun spot to hang out. I've heard lots of great things about it from folks at church."

His chiseled jaw tightened almost reflexively, then slowly eased as if he was making a concerted effort to relax. "Good to know."

His clipped response warned her that she'd misstepped, and she frowned. "Did I say something wrong?"

"Course not."

Any fool could see that he didn't mean what he'd said, but she decided to let the matter drop. She didn't want to start an argument with someone who had the power to help her make a stable home for Parker and get her new business off the ground. "I'd like to rent this place for three months, with an option to buy when the lease runs out. That gives me a chance to get all my ducks in a row before making a huge commitment I might end up regretting."

"Yeah, I hear you," he said with a wry grin. "Wish I could've done that with my ex-wife."

It was Erin's turn to gawk. "You were married?"

"For more than a year. Sherry and I were about as different as two people could be, but there was something about her." He punctuated the very personal revelation with a rueful grin. "We both gave it our best shot, but eventually she decided I wasn't worth the trouble. Considering the way my parents ended up, I don't know why I thought I could make it work."

For Erin, the situation was exactly the opposite. Her parents' marriage had been full of love and laughter right up until the day her father died. That was why she was so picky about her relationships. If it wasn't wonderful, she wasn't interested. Which explained why, at twenty-eight, she was a frequent bridesmaid but had never walked down the aisle herself. "Sometimes people change when we're not looking, and it's smarter to admit that and move on."

"Is that what happened to you and whoever's heart you broke last?"

"You just assume that's how it ended?" When he grinned, she couldn't help smiling in return. "That's very flattering, but actually it was the opposite. He claimed our relationship suffered because I was so preoccupied with Parker, but I got the feeling that wasn't the whole story."

"You were probably too much for him from the get-go. Some guys have no clue what to do with a strong, intelligent woman like you."

She appreciated the boost to her ego, especially since it had come from someone who had no reason to sugarcoat things for her. "Whatever the reason, it wasn't fun."

"I can relate to that. The last six months of our marriage were the worst time of my life." He paused, and his eyes filled with misery. "Until Mom's stroke, anyway. I guess that takes first prize now."

Cam had always been the capable type, top five in his graduating class and an all-star point guard and wide receiver throughout high school. Because he'd had so much going for him, he'd been arrogant to the point of being downright cocky. He'd finally come up against something he couldn't defeat, and Erin's heart went out to him.

Reaching over, she rubbed his arm in sympathy. "I'm sorry for the reason, but your mom and Natalie must be glad you're here. They're proud of those big construction jobs you've been doing, but they must like having you around for more than just a quick visit."

"So they keep telling me, but I have a life to get back to. My boss has been great, but he can't keep my spot open forever. I'm staying just long enough to get the café and this building in shape to sell so Mom will have some financial security. After that, Alex and Nat should be able to handle whatever needs to be done."

Always the practical one, Erin thought sadly. Sentimental as a buzz saw, Cam had never been the emotional type, and clearly his divorce hadn't helped any in that department. More than once, she'd suspected that his lack of empathy came from becoming the man of his family when he was twelve. That was the year his father, David, walked away from his wife and children and never looked back.

Mentioning that now probably wouldn't go

over well, so she kept the observation to herself. "Does that mean we have a deal?"

"Yeah. It's not like I've got buyers lined up outside my door or anything." The gloom in his eyes lifted ever so slightly, and he gave her a wry grin. "At least with you I know what I'm getting into."

"That's the spirit," she teased, lightly knuckling his chin. "I'm assuming your sister's got a lease form we can use to make this arrangement legal."

"No doubt."

"How much rent are you planning to charge me?" He named a figure, and she blinked at him. "Is that for all three months?"

"Funny. What were *you* thinking?" She countered, and he winced as if he was in serious pain. "You're killing me with that. Be reasonable."

In truth, she'd anticipated the pushback, so she made a show of reconsidering the price even though she'd purposefully gone in low. She might not have a fancy college degree, but one thing she'd learned from all the court cases she'd documented for the judge was how to negotiate. For her, getting the numbers right could be the difference between being financially secure for six months or an entire year. With a new business on the horizon, those six extra months could bend an outright failure into a modest success.

"Okay, how 'bout this?" she suggested in a brisk but friendly tone she hoped would appeal to him. "I'll split the difference between your rent figure and mine. You leave the For Sale sign on the building, and if someone else shows interest in it we'll talk about making a change."

After a few moments he offered his hand, and they shook to seal their bargain. Erin's previously cautious enthusiasm began bubbling, and she asked, "Can I paint the walls any color I want?"

"Now you're pushing."

He hadn't seen anything yet, she thought with a grin. But since he'd given her what she wanted for a price she could live with, she was willing to overlook his grumbling. "Do you have time to go see Natalie now?"

"Sure." She started to pull her hand back, but to her surprise, he held on, reeling her closer until they were barely a step apart. "One thing, Kinley."

"What's that?"

"No pink."

She liked having her old nemesis on the ropes this way, making him wonder what she might do to his precious building. Giving him her sweetest smile, she met his dark gaze with a direct one of her own.

"No promises."

Chapter Two

What a situation this had turned out to be, Cam groused to himself while he signed the papers that would connect Erin to him, at least in a professional way. He wasn't crazy about being a landlord, but he was pragmatic enough to recognize that his sister was right this time. Renting the empty building was better than continuing to front the costs with little hope of shedding them until spring.

Maybe, if business at Erin's pet shop took off, his first—and hopefully last—tenant would buy the place and he'd be one step closer to leaving Oaks Crossing behind him for good.

"So, when can I start moving in?" Erin asked, looking from Natalie to Cam with a hopeful expression. "I'd love for Parker and me to be able to start out next year in our new apartment."

"That's only a few days away," Natalie pointed out.

"No time like the present," Erin replied enthusiastically, reminding him of how he'd always admired the energy she seemed to have an endless supply of.

He suddenly realized that the two of them were staring at him expectantly, waiting for him to answer. Hoping to cover his lapse in manners, he dredged up a compliant smile. It would only be a few days before the lease officially began, and what could go wrong? "Sure. Whatever you want."

"Will your brothers be giving you a hand?" Natalie asked.

"Not if I can help it. They never listen to me, so it'll be easier and much less aggravating to do it myself."

"That's a lot of stairs to navigate," Natalie commented, giving Cam one of those nudging looks that he'd always thought women must practice in a mirror so they'd be ready to use for an occasion like this one.

When he refused to bite, her mild expression cooled into an icy glare that told him she meant business. After a few seconds, he had to admit she had a point. Moving an entire household was a lot for one person to manage, and any guy worth knowing wouldn't leave a woman to handle such a huge job alone. "I can give you a hand getting packed up and moved, if you want."

That made Erin laugh. "Like you're gonna listen to me any better than my brothers would."

"Suit yourself." Quite honestly, he was disappointed by her reaction. He wanted to be accommodating, but trying to do the right thing had earned him a virtual slap in the face.

"Hang on a minute." She considered him with a pensive look. "It would go a lot faster with the two of us. Do you still have that old pickup of yours?"

"Course I do. They don't make 'em like that anymore."

"Meaning no air-conditioning, power steering or functioning gas gauge," Natalie teased from behind her desk.

"Less complicated means less things to worry about," he informed her with a grin. "Plus, when something breaks I can fix it myself. These days, even the best mechanic needs a fancy computer to tell him what's wrong with a car."

Erin rolled those pretty green eyes and sighed. "You sound like my big brother. Mike's always complaining about how impossible it is to repair anything made in the last ten years."

"It's a conspiracy to make us all buy new stuff."

"Yeah, he says that, too."

Their discussion of modern convenience seemed to be over, and then out of nowhere he heard himself ask, "What do *you* think?"

He hadn't meant to say that out loud, but since he had, he did his best to look mildly interested in her answer. Erin had never been anything more to him than his buddy Drew's annoying younger sister. But this morning, Cam had glimpsed a different side of her that he hadn't noticed before. She'd always been sassy and too smart for her own good.

Now he knew firsthand what was most important to her and how she used that keen intelligence to get what she wanted. Employing a reasonable, logical argument, she'd convinced him to go along with something that only yesterday he couldn't have imagined himself agreeing to.

Despite the fact that he'd been forced to give in, Cam had to acknowledge that he was impressed by her tenacity.

"I'm partial to old things myself," she replied. "They've been around a long time, and I think they deserve to be taken care of."

"Not so much a fan of shiny and new?"

In response, she held out one of her beat-up

work boots for him to see. Chuckling, he took his copy of their lease from Natalie's desk and handed the other to Erin. "Gotcha. So, when did you wanna get started?"

"Yesterday."

The quick response was so like the determined girl he recalled that he couldn't keep back a laugh. Opening the office door for her, he bowed slightly as he held it open. "Ladies first."

"You can save your breath," she informed him as she flounced past him and out of the office. "Those fake manners of yours don't fool me."

"What makes you think they're fake?"

"I know you," she shot back. Fortunately, she'd kept her voice down so the other folks on the sidewalk couldn't hear the venom in her tone. "You haven't changed a bit since you dated your way through the cheerleading squad in high school."

"I was a football player," he joked. "It wasn't my fault the girls came with the uniform."

"Whatever."

She was pointedly ignoring him, even when he stopped and tugged her to a halt. When she looked up at him, he saw a bitterness that made him wish he could undo whatever he'd done to put it there. "You know I was only kidding, right?"

"Of course you were," she spat back, as if the words tasted sour on her tongue. "You never took me seriously back then, so why start now?"

"I never took you seriously because you hated me."

"I hated you because you never took me seriously."

He opened his mouth for a sly comeback, then thought better of it. After all, they were going to be neighbors for at least the next three months. It would go better for both of them if they laid their less-than-glorious past to rest.

Holding up the papers he'd so reluctantly signed, he summoned patience into his tone. "We're all grown up now, and that's how I see you. We're doing business together, aren't we?"

"Because you don't have a choice, not because you think it's a good idea."

They were finally getting somewhere, he thought. Lightly grasping her shoulders, he met her angry gaze with a calm one of his own. "Trust me, Erin. If I was the slightest bit worried that you were a bad risk, I wouldn't have agreed to lease you that building. If it makes you feel any better, my foot-dragging was totally personal. It had nothing to do with you."

"You're sure?"

"Absolutely." Letting her go, he stepped back and dredged up a wry grin. "Still hate me?"

Batting her eyelashes in a gesture totally out of character for her, she gave him an exaggerated Southern-belle smile. "Not as much."

"Give it time, darlin'," he teased in a heavy drawl as they continued down the walk. "Knowing me, it won't be long till I do something to make you mad."

Boy, did he call that one.

"Are you trying to drive me crazy?" Erin demanded when she saw how Cam was packing Great-Grandma Kinley's china. Snatching the Bubble Wrap from him, she demonstrated on a plate that she took from the small hutch. "Wrap the whole thing twice, then set it down flat in the box. They're very fragile, and if you put them on end, the rims might get damaged."

"Okay."

"These came all the way from Ireland on a sailing ship," she persisted in frustration. "It would be a shame if they couldn't survive moving from one side of Oaks Crossing to the other."

"Sorry. I should've been more careful."

It was the uncharacteristically humble tone that convinced her that his apology was sincere. Once her frantic, record-setting pace had been interrupted, she decided they could both use a breather. Carefully putting the heirloom dish into the padded moving carton, she turned to him and smiled. "Time for a break. I've got coffee and water, and I think there's some cherry pie in the fridge."

His gloomy expression brightened considerably. "Maggie's cherry pie?"

"Of course. Mom made an extra for Parker and me and sent it home with us after Christmas dinner. Help yourself."

Her everyday dishes were already packed, but the silverware organizer sat on the counter waiting for a box. Her resourceful helper tore off a couple of paper towels and served up a piece of pie for each of them.

Biting into a mouthful of his, he hummed in appreciation. "Your mother's a genius when it comes to food. Must be an Irish thing."

"It's supposed to be," Erin acknowledged with a laugh. "I guess it skips a generation or something, because my niece Abby loves to cook but I can't stand it."

"You're good at other things."

The compliment caught her off guard, and she gave him a long, curious look. "Did you just say something complimentary about me?"

"Huh," he commented, as if it hadn't oc-

curred to him until she mentioned it. "I guess
so. Can't imagine what came over me."

Mischief sparked in his eyes, and she
couldn't help laughing. "Are you really as bad
as all that, or is it just an act?"

"You tell me."

While they stared at each other, the playful
gleam deepened to something she wasn't sure
she liked. The trouble was, she wasn't sure she
didn't like it, either. Rattled by her conflicting
emotions, she fell back on her usual defense.
Tossing her head defiantly, she said, "I think
you just want people to assume you're bad so
they won't hassle you."

"Then why do *you* keep hassling me?"

"Because I'm not afraid of you," she informed him, staring him down to make her
point more clearly. "I never was, and I never
will be."

The corner of his mouth quirked in an almost smile, and he seemed to take the revelation in stride. "Good to know."

It was nuts, but she couldn't shake the impression that the mellow timbre of his deep
voice was actually making the glassware on
the table vibrate. "I'm glad you're happy. Now,
can we please get back to work?"

"Yes, ma'am."

Eager to get away from him, she turned and

headed for Parker's bedroom to pack up his clothes. While she strode down the hallway, she felt Cam's eyes following her as she went.

What is he thinking? she wondered before she could stop herself. Because, really, she had no business wondering anything about her enigmatic landlord. After he helped her move all this stuff, they'd probably only see each other long enough to trade the occasional "good morning" or for her to complain that there was no hot water. If all went well, she'd buy his building and shove him several steps closer to returning to the life in Minnesota he was so eager to resume.

Logical and practical, that line of thinking should have reassured her. But for some reason it made her feel sad.

"Is this one ready?"

Cam's voice startled her, and she nearly jumped out of her skin when he appeared beside her. "Are you trying to give me a heart attack?"

"Not hardly." He cocked his head with a curious look. "Where were you just now? You looked like you were a million miles away."

Wonderful. Now he was worrying about her. She really had to get it together, or he'd think she was turning into a flake. Not that she cared one whit about his opinion, of course. She just didn't want to give him a reason to doubt that she was responsible enough to pay her rent on time every month.

"Just thinking about what color to paint Parker's new room." On a whim, she decided to have some fun torturing her new landlord. "He really likes black."

Cam glowered at that. "Not a chance. You know how tough it is to cover—" Pausing, he gave her a long, assessing look. "You're messing with me, aren't you?"

"Just a little. It's fun."

"For you," he growled, heaving the large box onto his shoulder as if it was full of feathers. "Truck or car?"

"Truck. Thank you." His shocked reaction to her comment made her laugh. "What?"

"You thanked me. Y'know, like you'd do with someone you don't hate."

"Tell you what," she suggested with a smile, "if you're nice to me, I'll be nice to you."

"I guess that could work. We could give it a shot, anyway."

"I'm willing if you are." That sounded way too personal, and she quickly added, "Since we're going to be neighbors and all."

Those dark eyes studied her for a few moments, then drifted away as if they didn't like what they saw. Without another word he headed into the hallway, and she heard his boots thumping down the front hall before the entryway door banged open and closed.

What on earth is his problem? she wondered angrily, snapping open another flat moving box and forming it into the right shape. While she packed the bedding and books Parker had collected, she went over her conversation with Cam in her mind, trying to determine where it had veered from lighthearted to slam-the-door.

When she realized it had been her reference to them being neighbors that set him off, she was puzzled. She was only trying to establish the fact that their connection to each other was professional, not personal. Since he'd been so clear about his aversion to serious relationships, she figured he'd be glad to know she felt the same way. Judging by his response, he was anything but glad. His swift turn from teasing to intense made no sense to her, and that brought her back to something that, as the only girl in a sea of overbearing brothers, she'd believed for most of her life.

Boys were stupid, and a smart girl never forgot that.

Cam ended up spending a good chunk of his day helping Erin.

He was shocked to discover that it was a

lot more enjoyable than he'd expected it to be when Natalie had volunteered him for pack and schlep duty. Even more surprising was the fact that every time he stopped by to check in at the café, things were running more or less smoothly.

"Sure, boss," Kyle assured him with a competent nod. "You put on extra staff to help with the after-holiday crowd, remember? Everything's going fine."

Lately, things had been going anything other than fine for him, and Cam couldn't quite believe the change was for real. "What's the word on the cooler?"

"Just a worn-out doohickey that had to be replaced. Fred didn't even charge you," the kid added with a grin. "Said to call it a late Christmas present."

The cavalier attitude rubbed Cam the wrong way, and he came close to ordering Kyle to pay the repairman, anyway. Then he thought again, reminding himself that he was in Oaks Crossing, not Minneapolis. Against all modern odds, Oaks Crossing was still the kind of place where neighbors helped each other out when they could. While he certainly owed Fred some kind of favor in return, Cam decided that trying to force the generous man to accept payment for his services would come across as rude. So, despite the fact that it bugged him, he opted to leave the situation as it currently stood.

"All right," he finally said, taking a last look around the orderly kitchen. "I'll be next door a while longer. Let me know if you need anything."

"Will do."

Baffled by the strange twists and turns his day had taken so far, Cam left the restaurant and grabbed the last of Erin's boxes from the bed of his truck. He hauled it upstairs and found her in the small living room, listening to a local country station and pulling together anything labeled Parker.

"What're you doing?" Cam asked as he set the box marked Kitchen Stuff on the breakfast bar. While he was at it, he discreetly bumped the volume knob on the small stereo so the music dropped to a more acceptable murmur. Erin gave him a knowing look but didn't say anything, so he counted that as a victory.

"Parker's hanging out with Abby at the farm today, and Mom's going to bring him by in—" she checked the oversize watch on her wrist "—an hour. I want his room to be ready when he gets here."

The gesture got his attention, and he went closer to get a better look at the rugged piece of jewelry. Nothing fancy, it was obviously designed for a man, with bold numbers inside a cloudy crystal that had seen better days. And then it hit him: it hadn't always been hers. "Is that your dad's watch?"

"Yeah." She tilted it toward her with a sad smile. "I used to like wearing it when I was a little girl, so he left it to me. I've worn it ever since."

"That's nice." While he appreciated her down-to-earth tribute, Cam couldn't help wishing that he and his father had shared the kind of relationship that made him want to do something similar. The truth was, David Stewart had left his son with nothing but icy hatred for the man who'd abandoned his wife and children because their life together hadn't turned out the way he'd planned.

Eager to embrace something more positive, Cam shouldered a box full of bedding and headed down the hallway. After a few moments' hesitation, he heard Erin sigh and start dragging another carton down behind him.

When he turned into the smaller bedroom, she called out, "No, the other one."

"That's the master," he argued, turning to face her. "It's got two windows and a much bigger closet. Plus, it faces Main Street with a view of the park instead of the brick wall from the building next door."

"I want Parker to have the brighter space," she insisted in a don't-argue-with-me tone. So, being a relatively intelligent man, Cam changed direction and hung a left.

As he carried the heavier pieces back for her, he couldn't help being awed by her selflessness. "Most women I know wouldn't have given up the walk-in closet, much less the pretty view outside, for anyone."

Erin shrugged. "I guess I'm not like the other women you've known."

Got that right, he nearly said before he stopped himself. The comment had a good chance of being taken the wrong way, and he didn't want to say anything that might suggest he was more impressed with his new tenant than he should be.

The pieces of Parker's twin bed were leaning against the wall, and when Cam started assembling the frame, he noticed the parts didn't quite fit but had been rigged to work as a set.

"What's up with this?" he asked, motioning to the glued-and-screwed posts.

"When Parker came to live with me, I didn't have a bed for him. The boys were tough on theirs, but Josh took them apart and scrounged enough pieces to make one good set."

"That's debatable," Cam commented with a scowl. Looking around the room and then at the enormous pile of things she intended to cram in here, he added, "This kid has a ton of stuff. Where are you gonna put everything?"

"I'll figure it out," she assured him, determination flaring in her eyes. "Contrary to what men like to believe, some women are perfectly capable of managing all kinds of things on their own."

Translation: I counted on a man once, and he let me down. While Cam's failed marriage helped him understand where she was coming from, the unexpected bite of her Irish temper set him back a step, and he raised his hands in a calming gesture. "Trust me, I'm not one of those guys. If I was ever stupid enough to have that attitude, Mom and Natalie would've set me straight years ago. Can I make a suggestion?"

Her eyes narrowed in suspicion, but she gave him a tentative nod.

"Let's start the new year out with a clean slate." Offering his hand, he said, "I'm Cam Stewart. Welcome to the building."

After a moment, she laughed and followed along. "Erin Kinley. Nice to meet you."

"So, I hear you've got a bunch of stuff to fit into this oversize closet of a bedroom," he went on, continuing the charade. "I can see you've got things under control up here, but would you be interested in some free help to boss around?"

"That would be great, if you're not too busy."

"Never too busy to lend a hand to a new neighbor," he assured her with a grin. "As a matter of fact, I've got a couple of old counter stools over at the café that'd work for your breakfast bar. Would you like me to bring 'em up here for you?"

She rewarded him with a pixie grin that told him he'd finally struck the right chord with her. "Sure. Thanks."

"Anytime."

As he trotted down the stairs, Cam congratulated himself on devising a way for Erin and him to set their less-than-friendly past to rest for good. It might seem goofy to someone else, but he acknowledged that his solution had done more than clear the air.

It had made a very serious woman smile. To his mind, there was nothing better than that.

By the time he found those stools buried under a pile of old furniture in the back corner of the basement storeroom, he'd nearly given up. They were dusty and laced with cobwebs, but after a quick hosing and drying, the sturdy chairs were ready to go. Just in time, too, because as he was delivering them to Erin, he spotted Maggie Kinley's familiar old SUV turning onto Main Street. He hurried upstairs, set the stools in place and was on his way out when he heard, "Where are you going?"

Turning, he found Erin standing outside Parker's room holding a pillow in one hand and some kind of outdoorsy pillowcase in the other. "I figured this is a family thing."

"You've been helping me all day long," she argued with a smile. "I think you deserve to see Parker's face when he finds out what we've been up to in here."

Something about the way she said "we" touched a part of him that he didn't often bother with. It was the shadowy, distant corner of his heart that still believed—however faintly—that his own company wasn't really enough for him, no matter how many times he insisted it was. Since there wasn't time for him to gracefully leave, he decided to let that part of him answer, just this once. "I'd like that, too. Thanks for thinking of it."

She gave him the kind of smile he'd never seen all those years he'd been tormenting her. Shy and sweet, it had a warm quality to it that made him smile back.

Footsteps on the stairs broke that brief, unexpected connection, and Cam retreated down the hallway with a vague comment about checking the drains in the bathroom. When it occurred to him that he meant to leave so Erin would have the spotlight, he was puzzled. It wasn't like him to give ground to anyone, and why he'd suddenly do it now was beyond him.

Maybe there was still a hint of Christmas spirit in the air, he mused before grinning at his own foolishness. Then again, it was as good an explanation as any.

"You mean, we're going to live here?" Parker asked, blue eyes shining with an emotion Erin couldn't quite identify. It could sometimes be hard to tell what he was feeling, since he seemed reluctant to get excited about things. Even at Christmas, he'd held back from tearing open his gifts the way Abby had, as if he was scared to let anyone know how he felt about his presents.

Her mother had come and gone, so it was up to Erin to put him at ease. "You remember we talked last month about moving into town when the judge retired, right?"

He nodded, and Erin forged ahead with a chipper attitude that was as much for her benefit as his. She recognized that she was taking a huge risk, starting a new business in a less-than-robust economy. If Pampered Paws failed, she didn't have a Plan B, and that kind of situation had always made her nervous. Now it was even more worrisome, because she had someone else relying on her. "Well, living over the pet store will make it easier for me to get it up and running quickly. Plus, you'll be closer to the town park where you and Abby like to play."

"Can I still go out to the farm?"

The anxiety in his soft voice just about broke her heart, and she realized that he'd assumed that in gaining one thing, he'd have to give up another that meant a lot to him. Countless times in the several months she'd been his foster mom, she'd silently cursed the people responsible for making this sweet, intelligent boy so fearful of losing what he loved.

Forcing a bright smile, she ruffled his hair. "Anytime you want. The horses and all the critters at the rescue center would miss you if you didn't go see them. Not to mention, Grammy would forget how to make oatmeal cookies if you weren't around to help her."

"No, she wouldn't," he replied with a shy smile. "Grammy knows how to make everything."

That tiny burst of confidence in her mother made Erin want to cheer. More than anything, Parker needed to have adults in his life that he could trust without question. That Mom had earned her way into his heart through baking didn't surprise Erin in the least. Between her own children and a small army of local kids, Mom had been doing it for as long as Erin could remember.

"Yeah, I guess you're right." She heard footsteps coming out of the bathroom, and in the hallway she saw Cam holding a faucet handle that had apparently broken loose. At his questioning look, she smiled and waved him in. "Parker, this is an old friend of the family, Cam Stewart. He was at Drew and Bekah's wedding, but he left before I could introduce you to him. He owns the Oaks Café."

"Actually, my mom does," Cam corrected her, addressing his comment to Parker as he offered his free hand. "It's good to meet you, Parker."

"Nice to meet you, too, sir," the boy responded quietly, avoiding eye contact while they shook hands. He was that way when he encountered anyone outside the family, and Erin reminded herself that while it was concerning, she had to be patient with him.

Cam, however, seemed to have other ideas. Setting the fixture on an unopened box, he hunkered down so he was on a level with the shy boy. An awkward silence settled over them, and Erin opened her mouth to fill the void. Catching her eye, Cam stalled her with a slight shake of his head.

Focusing back on Parker, she noticed that he seemed to be waiting for something. Erin couldn't begin to grasp what was going on, but instinct told her that it was important, so she kept quiet and watched the two of them.

After what felt like forever, Parker lifted his chin and gazed thoughtfully at Cam, assessing this new adult to determine whether or not he could be trusted. For his part, Cam didn't say a word, just kept staring back as if he intended to do it the rest of the day if that's what it took for Parker to be comfortable around him. And then, just when she was beginning to think it was all pointless, the most amazing thing happened.

"Is that your old truck out front?" Parker asked.

"Yeah, it is. It's a fifty-six Ford pickup my granddad and I restored when I was in high school."

"It's real nice. You did a good job."

Cam grinned at him. "Thanks."

"Does it have three gears or four?"

Standing, Cam fished his keys out of his jeans pocket and dangled them in front of Parker. "Why don't you come check it out for yourself?"

The kid who never spoke more than a sentence or two to a new acquaintance flashed a questioning look at Erin. "Can I?"

A surge of joy threatened to pop out of her mouth, and she swallowed to keep it in check. "Sure. You boys have fun."

Clearly delighted, Parker all but ran from the apartment and started pounding down the stairs before Cam even stood up.

Because she could no longer contain her excitement, she beamed up at him. "I'm not sure what you did, but thank you."

"I didn't do anything, but you're welcome."

"Modesty from Cam Stewart?" she teased with a smirk. "That's a first."

That got her a decidedly sour look. "Don't give me a hard time. I'm trying to be agreeable."

"Amazing. I didn't think you had it in you."

"Yeah, yeah, yeah," he grumbled on his way out. "Don't rub it in."

Laughing, she closed the door behind him and sneaked over to the front window, standing out of sight to get a view of the male-bonding scene unfolding on the curb outside. Cam motioned to Parker, then said something that prompted the boy to open the driver's door and climb into the cab of the vintage blue pickup. He grasped the steering wheel like a race car driver, sawing the wheel back and forth while a laughing Cam got in beside him. Boys and their toys, she thought with a smile. You had to love it.

Satisfied that her son was in good hands, she turned up the volume on the stereo and got back to work.

Leaving Erin and Parker to get settled in their new apartment, Cam headed for his mother's house. Since her second stroke, he and Natalie had split the days, her checking on Mom in the morning, while Cam stopped by in the afternoon and then spent the night after closing the restaurant. A home-care nurse covered the hours in between so their mother was never alone.

Although the cost of such expert care was high, they'd both agreed that it was the best thing for her. Because Natalie had a family of her own, Cam had been covering the majority of the bills himself. It was draining his savings account at an alarming rate, but until all of her doctors declared her out of danger, he was committed to doing it. He recognized that he wasn't able to control everything, but if anything happened to her that he could have stopped, he'd never forgive himself.

As he drove through town, he allowed himself a self-pitying sigh. His life in Minnesota had been just what he'd always wanted. Following his divorce, he'd embraced his second chance at bachelorhood with gusto, working hard every day, even taking building design classes a couple of nights a week to expand his professional options for when he got too old to meet the physical demands of hands-on construction work.

Being responsible to—and for—no one but himself was a great way to live, and he'd decided that he just wasn't cut out for anything more.

His preference for an uncomplicated existence had made it tough for him to come dragging back to Oaks Crossing, but he couldn't keep enjoying himself when his mother and sister needed him. That was his father's way, Cam thought with a grimace in the rearview mirror. When in doubt, he always chose the opposite of what that selfish weasel had done. No matter how hard it was, he'd never allow himself to drop low enough to follow in that traitor's footsteps.

As Cam turned onto Cherry Street, he had to wait for a young mother pushing a stroller while she called to a toddler lagging a few yards behind her. This was the oldest part of town, filled with graceful homes built for raising large families. Christmas lights still hung

from windows and outdoor trees, and walk-
ways led to front porches with wreaths on the
front doors and garlands hanging from the railings.

When was the proper time to take those
down, anyway? Cam wondered as he continued down the street. Natalie and her husband,
Alex, had helped decorate their mother's house
at the beginning of December, but she hadn't
mentioned when the stuff should come down.
Whatever his sister's answer on that one, Cam
suspected he'd be doing that job by himself.
Putting everything up was fun, and there were
always plenty of hands willing to pitch in.
Packing it away, not so much.

As he turned into the driveway, he noticed
an unfamiliar sedan with Michigan plates
parked next to the nurse's red hatchback. The
driver was standing beside the car, staring at
the house as if he was trying to decide whether
or not he was in the right place. When Cam's
truck door slammed shut, the stranger turned,
clearly startled by the sound.

In a single breath, Cam's temper spiked to
eight on the Richter scale.

"What do you think you're doing here?" he
spat out, striding over to block the man's way
up the front steps.

"Hello, Cameron," his father replied with a

deferential nod. "I wasn't sure you'd remember me."

Only his mother used his full name anymore, and hearing it from someone he despised only fanned his anger. "You walked out on a family who needed you. That's not something I could forget."

"I know, and I don't blame you for hating me."

Cam swallowed a rush of curses that would have made a seasoned sailor blush. "What are you doing here?"

"I heard about Bridget's stroke."

"Which one?"

To his satisfaction, his father paled. "There's been more than one?"

"Two, actually. How did you find out?"

"Your aunt Connie emailed me just before Christmas," he explained, bowing his head in something that looked like shame. When he lifted it, he fixed a pleading look on Cam. "I had no idea things were so bad, or I would have come sooner."

"There wasn't much point in that," Cam snarled, folding his arms defiantly. "I'd just have run you off then instead of now."

"We never divorced, so she's still my wife," his father pointed out, showing a bit of backbone. "I have a right to see her."

Not a chance, Cam wanted to growl. Instead, he kept his cool and said, "This is Douglas property, and Granddad left it to Mom, not you. You have a right to leave before I call the sheriff."

"That's not fair."

In response, Cam pulled the cell phone from the front pocket of his jeans and started punching numbers.

"All right, you win." Holding up his hands, their unwelcome visitor backed toward his car. "I'm making a circuit of the area and will be coming back through here the first week in January. After that, I'll be staying at the B and B outside of town, and I'm not going anywhere until I see my wife."

"Looking for a job?"

"Actually," his father retorted, taking out a business card and holding it out to him, "these days, I'm the owner."

Natural curiosity prodded Cam to take the card, which read *David Stewart, Management Consultant*. Scottish pride kept him in his obstinate stance, glaring unmercifully at the man who seemed to think he could just stroll back into their lives as if he belonged there.

"You remind me of your Grandpa Douglas, God rest him," his father lamented, shaking his head. "He was stubborn and unforgiving, too."

"He was a great man, and he was there for

us every day until he died. He'd never even consider bailing on his family."

"Grudges are a heavy burden to haul around with you, son."

"Don't ever call me that," Cam snarled. "As far as I'm concerned, I lost my father years ago."

Before he could do something that would land him in jail, he forced himself to turn away and stalk up the porch steps. Behind him, he heard a heavy sigh and a car door closing. Once the sound of the engine began to fade, he glanced back to see the car slowly making its way toward Main Street.

Wonderful, he thought as he opened the front door to go inside. And he'd thought the day had *started* badly.

"Hello, Cam." His mother's nurse greeted him from the kitchen doorway. "How are you today?"

He wasn't sure how to answer that, so he sidestepped the question. "Wondering when it's appropriate to take down Christmas decorations."

The cheerful woman laughed. "When your mother says it's okay."

"Makes sense." Glancing toward the living room, he quietly asked, "How's she doing today?"

"I've never had the joy of caring for a patient with such a marvelous attitude."

Translation: the same. Cam fought off a dejected sigh and forced a smile. "That's nice to hear. Is she awake?"

"And waiting for dinner with you. The café sent over a delicious-smelling chicken and dumplings meal for the two of you, and it's keeping warm in the oven. You look beat," she added in a concerned tone. "Is there anything I can do before I go?"

"No, thanks. I've got it from here."

She gave him a doubtful look but thankfully didn't press him for details. After the infuriating run-in with his father, he wasn't exactly in the mood to be sociable.

"Well, all right. Call me if you need anything."

"Thanks."

After walking her out, he took a moment to regain his usual calm before talking to Mom. Resting a hand on the antique door, he looked down at the faded floral rug that had been in the entryway since long before he'd been born. Old and solid like the oak trees that surrounded it, the house had been built by one of the founders of the town and owned by his descendants ever since.

Mom's current condition might be the end

of that run, Cam mused with a frown. If he couldn't figure out a way to pull the family business out of the ever-deepening hole that he'd found it in, selling the homestead could be their only way out of debt. He hated to think of that happening on his watch, but modern finances didn't always mesh with keeping a family's history intact. Much as it pained him, he had to be practical.

Explaining it to Mom would be another thing altogether. For now, he put that out of his mind and plastered a nonchalant grin on his face before sauntering into the living room like he didn't have a care in the world.

"Hey there," he said smoothly, leaning in to kiss her cheek. "How's my favorite girl?"

Eyes that used to be a clear blue had a cloudy tinge to them, and it took her a few seconds to focus on him. When she did, the unaffected left side of her face crinkled with what now passed for her smile. "Better."

Because her speech was so limited, these days she kept her end of conversations short. It killed him to see his formerly bubbly mother reduced to this, but he held out hope that her ongoing therapy would unlock whatever ability she still had and make the most of it.

Reaching for something positive, he landed on the only thing all day that had made him smile. "Erin Kinley's gonna rent the old general store building from us. She and I signed the papers with Natalie this morning."

Her smile deepened a little at the news. "That's good. Living there?"

"Yeah, with her foster son, Parker. Have you met him?" She shook her head, but her expression brightened slightly, prompting him to go on. "He's had a tough time, but he seems like a great kid. Really liked my truck."

"Heard some things," she said in a halting voice, clearly hunting for the right words. "Poor boy."

With the precarious state her own health was in, that she could feel sympathy for someone else's problems made Cam feel ashamed for pitying his own situation. "She's opening a pet store, aiming to have it ready to go before spring. I offered to design and build the fixtures she needs, so that oughta help move things along."

"My Cam," Mom approved, extending a trembling hand to pat his arm. "Such a good boy."

Her praise hit him hard, and he had to swallow the lump that suddenly clogged his throat. Accustomed to working with a crew of tough-as-nails guys, he wasn't used to having a softer touch in his life, and he had to admit it was kind of nice. "Thanks. Are you ready for dinner?"

Shaking her head, she pinned him with an alarmingly alert stare. "Who was here?"

Assuming she'd been asleep during his father's unwelcome stop, Cam swallowed a curse. "No one." She gave him a chiding look, and he relented with a frown. "Fine. Your husband came by, and I told him it was a bad time for a visit."

There would never be a good time, but Cam figured it was best to keep that opinion to himself. He didn't want to upset her any more than necessary.

"Why?" she asked.

"You mean, why did he come, or why did I send him away?"

"Both."

Cam filled her in on the little he knew, then remembered the business card he'd jammed into his pocket. He fished out the crumpled paper and showed it to her. Then, to his amazement, she took it from him and stared at it for several long moments.

"You should call him," she finally said.

When she got tired, her speech began to slur a bit, and he assumed he'd misunderstood. "I'm sorry, Mom. What did you say?" She repeated it, and he scowled. "Not a chance."

"Please?" Fixing him with a trusting look, she gave him another half smile. "At least think about it."

Cam's instinct was to refuse outright, then list the many reasons they all had for avoiding contact with the man who'd abandoned them when he'd come to the decision that his family was more of a burden than he cared to shoulder. Just as he was about to launch his argument, though, Cam noticed something in his mother's gaze.

Fatigue had begun to set in, and her ability to focus on him was starting to fade. But somewhere in the lines of her face he saw a trace of her old determination. It was the kind of look she'd given him when he was a teenager bent on defying her just for the fun of testing her limits. Seeing it now bolstered his flagging hope that in time she'd recover from this devastating blow and be herself again.

"You want to see him, don't you?" he asked.

"Not if it hurts you."

Meaning she wanted it for herself but wouldn't sacrifice Cam's peace of mind to get it. For the life of him, he couldn't begin to understand why she felt so strongly about reconnecting with a man who'd neglected her for so long. His father wouldn't be back in town for a few days yet, which gave him some time to mull over the situation and make a decision.

"Okay, Mom," he finally gave in, covering her frail hand with one of his own. Giving a gentle squeeze, he forced a smile. "For you, I'll think about it. But don't tell anyone I gave up so easy. I've got a reputation, y'know."

That got him a faint laugh, and she murmured a thank-you.

"You're welcome. Meantime, I'm starving. How 'bout you?"

"Smells good."

"Sure it does," he replied in a chipper tone he hoped disguised how he was really feeling. "Lena still uses your recipe at the Oaks, and it's a big hit."

His mother beamed at the mention of her old friend, who happened to be a fantastic cook. While he got their dinner together, Cam searched his memory for snippets of town news that he thought might interest her. He knew he wasn't the most entertaining person in the world, but Oaks Crossing was full of characters ranging from quirky to borderline insane.

All he had to do was cherry-pick some of the mindless gossip he heard at the café on a daily basis. Apparently, the busybodies he'd spent most of his life resenting served a purpose, after all. Who knew?

Chapter Three

Someone was going to die.

She'd start with whoever thought it was a good idea to start hammering at—Erin squinted at the clock on her phone—seven on a Wednesday morning. Thankfully, Parker had spent the night at a friend's house and wasn't here to be rudely awakened by the busy beaver hacking away downstairs.

Recognizing that her tattered sweats and "Whatever" T-shirt were hardly the right outfit for this particular confrontation, she yanked an oversize Cincinnati football jersey overtop and stormed down the stairs to restore some peace. Her bare feet stomping down the wooden steps didn't make much of an impact, and by the time she reached the first floor she had a good head of steam going.

Seeing who she had to thank for her early

wake-up call didn't help settle her temper even the slightest bit. "Cam!"

Obviously startled, he jerked his head around and stared at her as if she was the last person he'd expected to find there. "Yeah?"

Reminding herself that cluelessness was a dominant male characteristic, she struggled not to scream at him. "Do you know what time it is?"

"About seven. Too early for you?"

"It's Christmas vacation." He gave her the blankest look she'd ever seen, and she realized that he needed more of an explanation than that. Without caffeine, the best she could dredge up was, "Sleeping in is part of the deal."

His sheepish expression was completely at odds with the cocky guy she remembered, and in her foggy state she actually thought it made him look cute. "Sorry. I don't have kids, so I didn't get that memo. Want me to come back later?"

"No," she answered on a yawn. "I'm awake now, and I've got tons to do myself. Want some coffee?"

The offer was clearly a surprise to him, and she had to admit she didn't know where the invitation had come from. She must be more tired than she thought. But it would be rude to extend it and then yank it back, so she tried to look okay with the idea.

"That'd be nice," he said, grinning over at her. "Can I make a suggestion first?"

"Sure."

"You might wanna turn your sweatshirt right side out so people can see more than just an outline of the tiger."

Erin glanced down to discover that she had indeed pulled her outer layer on inside out. Seeing as the rest of her life felt totally discombobulated these days, the mistake fit right in. She set it to rights, then took a moment to check out what he'd been up to. There were a lot of markings on the walls and the scarred wooden floor, measurements for the furnishings they'd briefly discussed yesterday.

Then she saw the gap in the ceiling and the pile of acoustic tiles that had fallen from it. "What happened?"

"I hate these drop ceilings," he grumbled. "I was poking around with a broom handle to make sure there weren't any soft spots, and that section just about fell on my head. I really think you'd be better off to pull the whole system down and either Sheetrock it or leave the beams exposed."

Erin craned her neck to get a better look through the hole. "What's up there?"

"The original oak beams, ductwork, stuff like that. These days, lots of folks paint the metalwork and either stain the wood or leave it natural. It's a cool look, and as a bonus it brings a lot more height to the space."

"Interesting."

Cam went over to the makeshift workbench he'd made using a wide board resting on two sawhorses. Taking a large set of drawings from the top, he brought them over to her and held them out for her to see. "I found the original plans in the office at the café. Up here—" he pointed "—it looks like they had four windows just a little ways down from where you're living. Back in the day, they probably used it as a storage loft. If the windows are still intact, we can open things up to let in a lot more light."

"That would be great." Erin was impressed, not only with his obvious knowledge but with the effort he'd already put into improving the neglected old building. "This is more than construction experience, though. Where did you learn all this design stuff?"

For the first time she was aware of, the arrogant bane of her existence actually looked shy. "I've been taking some building design and historical restoration classes at a college up in St. Paul. I've always loved these old buildings, and I think it'd be cool to have a job bringing them back to the way they used to be."

"Very cool," Erin agreed. "And obviously a great use of your talents."

That got her a very suspicious look. "Did you just say something nice about me?"

"Don't be dense. I did that the other day at least once."

"Yeah, but I thought that was 'cause you wanted something from me."

She folded her arms and glared at him. "Do you honestly think that's the only time I can be pleasant?"

"In my experience, that's how women are."

"Then your experience has been sorely lacking."

A slow, lazy grin spread across his tanned features. "Y'know, I think maybe you're right."

"Of course I am," she retorted, pushing past him to head upstairs. "Now, come up here and help me find my coffeemaker."

She heard a rumble of laughter behind her. "You mean, Miss Organization lost something in the move?"

A less-than-civil comeback was perched on the tip of her tongue, and it took the rest of her fleeting patience to keep it to herself. When they reached the top of the stairs, he let out a low whistle. "Did a tornado touch down yesterday? It didn't look like this last time I was here."

"This place is smaller than our old one," she shot back, glaring at the stacks of boxes she still had to sort through. "I have to find a spot for everything."

He glanced down the hallway and into Parker's room. "Looks like everything's perfect in there."

"I started in there," she explained while she shoved aside unmarked boxes, hunting for one labeled Appliances. She'd packed it first, when she'd been taking her time and arranging their things just so. "He'll be back at lunchtime, and I wanted to make sure his stuff is ready for him when he gets here."

"Sounds like a mom," Cam said in a quiet voice that pulled her attention away from her search. She almost fell over when he smiled at her. "When he was checking out my truck, he couldn't tell me enough about how great you are. You're making a huge difference in that kid's life, and under the circumstances, that can't be easy."

"It's not," she acknowledged soberly, then felt a little smile creeping in. "Thanks for the compliment."

"Not a compliment at all," he corrected her in a firm, matter-of-fact tone. "An observation. Flattery's really not my style anymore. Gets me in too much trouble."

The unexpected confession made her laugh. "Seriously? And all these years I thought you were the master."

"Things change," he said with a frown. "People change."

Erin honestly had no idea if her old nemesis had changed or not, but she couldn't deny that he'd treated her better than she'd expected. So, in the spirit of détente, she decided to give him the benefit of the doubt. At least for now.

"I guess you're right about that." Casting around, her eyes lit on the box she'd foolishly tucked into the corner farthest from the tiny galley kitchen. "Oh, there it is!"

She started pushing her way toward it when he stopped her with a hand on her arm. "Just stay there. I'll get it."

Being a single parent and independent by nature, Erin was used to taking care of everyday things herself. Her large, loving family was a wonderful safety net if she needed them, but she found a lot of satisfaction in fending for herself. As the only Kinley girl, she considered her three overbearing brothers both a blessing and a curse, depending on the day.

When they were growing up, she'd lumped Cam Stewart right in there with them. But now they were business partners, and she had to learn how to work with him. Allowing him to retrieve her gourmet coffeemaker was a small step in that direction, and she congratulated herself on keeping the peace by simply keeping her mouth shut.

"Thank you." Tearing open the box, she set the gleaming machine on the breakfast bar and in no time the scent of vanilla-and-nut-flavored caffeine filled the small living space. She handed a cup to her guest and indulged in a long whiff of her own before taking a sip. "Ahh…that's the stuff."

"I wouldn't spit it out, that's for sure."

"Oh, stop it," she teased in an overdone Southern-honey voice, fanning her face with her hand. "You'll turn my head."

He laughed, then angled a look at her. "I don't remember you being so funny."

"You were too busy yanking my chain to notice much else."

"Yeah, I guess." Suddenly his expression shifted to something much less humorous. "Things were a lot simpler back then, weren't they?"

Sensing that he wasn't referring to high school pranks, Erin set down her mug and gave him her full attention. "It's been tough on you, being there for your mom all the time."

"Natalie's got her hands full with Sophie."

"I wasn't talking about Natalie," Erin reminded him gently. "I was talking about you. It's not easy to put your own life on hold and take care of someone else."

Her sympathy seemed to be getting through the brave front he was trying to maintain, and he dragged his fingers through his hair with a deep sigh. Staring down at his coffee, he admitted, "No, it's not, but I'm doing my best."

"Of course you are. You always do, because that's who you are. You keep at something until you figure out how to make it work."

"This is different." Lifting his eyes to hers, he confided, "I don't think Mom's ever gonna be the way she was."

Accepting the truth was important to his own well-being, and Erin searched for a way to bring him some small measure of comfort. "Maybe not, but you and Natalie can help her make the most of what she has now. When I last saw her in church, it was obvious that she adores her granddaughter, so when she's up to it, spending time with Sophie will be great for her. God sends kids down to us because they have a way of making everything better, no matter how bad it looks."

Silence.

The apartment was so quiet she could hear

the slight hum of the coffeemaker's warming system. Open and optimistic only a few moments before, Cam's expression darkened ominously as barely restrained fury simmered in his eyes. Setting his half-empty mug on the counter, he turned away from her and made a beeline for the staircase. "Thanks for the coffee."

His sudden turn of mood baffled her, and she called after him, only to be ignored. Irked by the cold shoulder, she tried again, this time adding a little temper for effect.

His hand on the old newel post, he angled a look back at her. "Yeah?"

"Did I say something wrong?"

His jaw tightened as if he was struggling to hold back a harsh response, and she said, "It's okay—be honest. I can take it."

Hesitating, he seemed to be trying to form an answer to the toughest question on Earth. Then he met her confused gaze with a cool one of his own. "God and I haven't been on speaking terms for a long time."

"Do you mind telling me why?"

As his look darkened even more, she thought he wasn't going to answer. Finally, in a strained voice, he explained. "When we were kids, we learned that if something was really important to us, we just had to ask God for it, and He'd make it happen. After my dad left, I prayed every night for him to come back, but he never did."

"That was his choice," Erin reasoned, feeling fresh sympathy for the anger he'd carried around with him all these years. "God doesn't go around making people do things against their will."

"What about us?" Cam persisted grimly. "Did we deserve to be treated like that, humiliated in front of the whole town?"

"No, but—"

He cut her off with a hand in the air. "I don't wanna discuss this with you. You still have your faith, but I lost mine. Let's leave it at that."

"I'm sorry, Cam. I didn't mean to upset you."

He gave her something between a grimace and a smile and headed down the stairs without another word. Watching him go, Erin wasn't sure what to think of his stunning revelation.

They'd attended the same church growing up, and she'd always assumed that he shared her beliefs. Her faith was an integral part of who she was, and it had never occurred to her that he might feel differently. Learning that he no longer had a relationship with God made her feel more than sorry.

It made her sad.

* * *

Cam didn't realize he'd been at it so long until Parker walked through the dingy, glass front door. With a backpack slung over his shoulder and a sleeping bag in his arms, he looked tired but happy.

"Hey there, sport," Cam greeted him lightly. "How was your sleepover?"

"Good," he answered with a yawn.

Cam chuckled. He remembered those days, when he and the Kinley boys would take over the parlor at the farm, build a fort out of sofa cushions and commandeer all the classic board games in the house. When they got tired of those, they'd stay up until all hours doing… well, nothing. "Sounds like you didn't sleep much. Did your friend have some new video games for you to check out?"

Parker nodded. "He got a bunch for Christmas, and we played 'em all. They were pretty cool, but I like mine better."

"Yeah? Why's that?"

"Because they're mine. I get to keep them and play them whenever I want. As long as my homework's done," he added earnestly. "That's the rule."

"It's a good one." Cam noticed Parker eyeing his toolbox with the kind of interest he'd felt himself as a boy. Thanks to Granddad, he'd always loved building things, taking a pile of random stuff and making something useful out of it. Something told him Parker shared that feeling. "I'm helping Erin with these repairs, and I could use an extra set of hands. Wanna help?"

"Sure." Parker slipped his backpack to the floor and dropped the sleeping bag on top of it. Clearly excited, he gazed up at Cam eagerly. "What do I do?"

"Take this—" Cam handed him the tabbed end of the tape measure "—and walk over to that far wall."

Parker complied, stopping when he reached the other end of the room. Then he came back and asked, "What now?"

"What number's on the tape?"

Something akin to panic seized the boy's face, and he visibly gulped. "You want me to do that? Isn't it kinda important to get it right?"

Cam was no expert on children, but he couldn't help thinking this kid was way too serious for someone his age. That was definitely something he could relate to. Then again, he hadn't had the best role model in his own father, so maybe he was wrong.

Following his gut had generally worked well for him, so he decided to try it now. "How old are you?"

"Eight."

"I'm thinking you learned your numbers in kindergarten. Am I right?"

Parker gave him a crooked grin. "Preschool."

"That makes you an expert, then." The boy nodded, and Cam grinned as he tapped the metal tape with his finger. "So look at the number and read it to me. Not so hard."

In a confident voice, his assistant rattled off a measurement that jibed with Cam's estimate of the distance. "Good job. That's what I got, too."

"How?"

"It's called a guesstimate. When you do a lot of carpentry and construction work, you kind of get a feel for stuff like this."

"So, you build things at your job? That's so cool. Grammy got me a building set for Christmas, and there's a whole book full of ideas." Glancing toward the original hand-drawn plans, he added, "Like those drawings."

"They're called blueprints," Cam explained as he let the tape recoil back into its housing. Strolling over, he motioned for Parker to join him. "This is how the builder knows how much material he needs, and what size it should be."

"Erin says you always need a plan."

Cam chuckled. "Yeah, that sounds like her."

Parker studied him with bright, intelligent

eyes. "She said you were friends with the Kinleys. Is that how you know so much about her?"

Cam had heard the fondness in his voice, and he wasn't entirely certain where it had come from. Grasping for a reasonable explanation, he replied, "I guess. We've known each other a long time."

"I wish I could've grown up here," Parker commented, looking out the front window with a wistful expression. "The people are real nice."

Nicer than the ones he'd known before Erin found him, Cam understood without being told. He didn't have a lot of experience with children in general, much less one from a troubled background like Parker, so he wasn't sure what to say. Finally, he settled on, "Yeah, they are."

"Is that why you came back?"

Drew had told him that Parker wasn't much of a talker, so Cam wasn't prepared for such a personal question. The fact that the shy boy had chosen him for a lengthy conversation made Cam feel proud in a way that he'd never experienced before.

He sat down on the rough-hewn bench that he was using to hold his tool box and patted the seat beside him. Seeing the boy gaze up at him with curiosity lighting his eyes gave Cam a strange feeling he couldn't have described if he'd tried. "Actually, I came because my mom got sick. She used to run the Oaks Café, and since she can't do that anymore, I'll be here helping out until she's feeling better."

Part truth, part wishful thinking. But the response got a somber nod from his new buddy. "Families should help each other, not hurt each other."

That was far too serious a thought for someone his age to come up with on his own, and Cam asked, "Who taught you that?"

"The Kinleys. Abby says I'm part of their family now, and they'll always be around if I need them. I like that."

Cam could easily imagine her saying something like that to lift the spirits of a child who'd been cast aside by his own family. He'd seen Erin's bubbly niece a few times and had noticed how outgoing and confident she was. In a few years, her father, Mike, would have his work cut out for him fending off the teenage boys lining up to take her out. Now that he thought about it, Cam felt sorry for all those boys. Mike was a bear on a good day. Cam hated to consider how tough the no-nonsense horse trainer would be on anyone who expressed a romantic interest in his little cowgirl.

"I had a lotta fun at Gallimore Stables over the years," Cam said with a smile. "What's your favorite thing to do?"

"I like taking care of the horses and all the animals at the rescue center. We're not allowed to help with the wild ones, but the puppies and kittens are fun. They really like to play."

"So you like old trucks, animals and building things. Anything else I oughta know?"

Parker mulled that over for a few seconds and shook his head. "I guess that's it."

"Okay, then, you're hired."

Cam stuck his hand out, and Parker gave him a quizzical look. "For what?"

"I thought you wanted to pitch in to get Erin's new store put together. Was I wrong?"

"I'm just a kid."

"I was your age when I started working with my granddad in his shop. He always said there was no better way to learn about something than to just jump in there and figure it out."

"I'm not allowed to use power tools," Parker cautioned in a wary tone.

"Got it. Whaddya say?"

This time, the boy slid his hand into Cam's and they shook to seal their deal. "What should I do first?"

The eagerness in his tone made Cam smile. "Go grab a snack and put on whatever you wear when you're doing barn chores. It's about to get messy down here."

"Yes, sir!"

Parker grabbed his overnight stuff and bolted up the stairs just as Erin was coming down. She flattened herself against the wall until he'd gone past and gave Cam a startled look. "What's gotten into him?"

"I just hired him as my apprentice. He's pretty psyched." Frowning, she opened her mouth, and he stopped her with a hand in the air. "Before you go all mom-ish on me, I know he's young and can't do a whole lot. I promise that anything I give him will be manageable for someone his age."

"I do not go 'mom-ish,'" she shot back, eyes snapping with the quick temper he remembered all too well. "It's my responsibility to keep him safe, Cam."

Parker's comments about the farm were still fresh in his mind, and he couldn't help grinning. "Does he ride horses with Abby?"

"Yes. Ponies," she added tartly, as if she'd figured out where his argument was headed.

"Does he ever roughhouse with your brothers or that monster golden retriever, Charlie?" This time, she kept quiet, and he knew he'd made his point. "I promise he won't be doing anything on his own. But since he's on vacation all week, I thought he might enjoy making some money while he learns things they don't teach in school anymore."

"Well…" Her eyes darted around the evolving construction zone as if they were searching for a reason to nix his idea. Finally, they settled on him and to his surprise, she smiled. "It's a great idea, and I know he'll have a blast. Thank you for thinking of it."

"No problem." That didn't seem like enough, and even though it wasn't like him to be so open with people, he decided to share what he was thinking. "It's obvious he's had a tough time, but he really loves you. It can't be easy being a single parent, but you're doing a great job."

"Mom's a big help," Erin said with a fond smile. "Abby started calling him her cousin right off, and the boys have been awesome."

"But?"

She gave him a long, assessing look, and he got the distinct feeling that she was measuring him for something. "He needs a guy that's kind of his, like a big brother or an uncle."

"You mean, like a father figure?" She nodded, and he frowned. "Considering the example I had, you really think I'm the right choice for that?"

"Just because your dad was a failure doesn't

mean you will be, too. In fact, I wouldn't be surprised if you wound up being a better father because you know what not to do."

The gentle sympathy in her voice caught him off guard, and he stared at her in amazement. Since she was from such a tight-knit family, he knew Erin didn't say things like that lightly. "You think I'll make a good dad?"

"Someday," she added hastily, blushing a little before turning away. "With the right person."

Stunned by her comments, he couldn't come up with a single rational thing to say. The awkward silence felt like it was dragging on, and he was desperately hunting for a way to end it when her cell phone rang.

She checked the caller ID with a worried look before answering. "Hi, Alice. Merry Christmas to you, too. I didn't think we were going to hear from you until after the New Year. What's up?"

Cam moved away to give her some privacy, gathering up his tools as quietly as possible so he wouldn't distract her from what appeared to be a very serious conversation. He glanced over several times, though, and each time she looked more upset. After several minutes, she ended the call and sank down onto the bottom step as if she couldn't stay on her feet another second longer.

"Erin?" She didn't seem to hear him, and he repeated her name a little louder. When those hazel eyes met his, they were filled with something he'd never seen in this brash, forthright woman. Fear.

Hurrying across the room, he settled on one knee in front of her and braced himself for the worst. "What's wrong? Who's Alice?"

After a long delay, Erin gave herself a visible shake and glanced up the stairs. "Not here."

She stood and walked toward the front door. As he followed her, it occurred to him that she was trying to make sure Parker wouldn't overhear their conversation. As upset as she was, it really impressed him that she could put aside her own distress in an attempt to spare her foster son's feelings.

When they were standing by the front display window, she answered him in a hushed voice. "That was Parker's social worker."

He realized she was trembling, and he steadied her with a hand on her shoulder. "What'd she say?"

"They found his mother, Lynn," Erin confided in a miserable whisper. "She's in a women's prison upstate, and she told Alice she wants to meet me."

That didn't sound like enough to put Erin in such a state, and he gently prodded. "There's something else. What is it?"

"She won't sign off on me continuing as Parker's foster mom until we talk face-to-face." After a long swallow, she fixed him with a desperate gaze. "What if she hates me? Or worse, what if she wants to give custody of him to someone who mistreated him before?"

Her voice trailed off into a strangled whisper, and tears welled in her eyes. In all the years he'd known her, Cam had never seen her cry. Not when she broke her arm falling out of an oak tree at a church picnic, or even when her date left the prom with someone else. Seeing her on the verge of it now made his heart twist in a way he'd never experienced in his life.

In self-defense, he pushed his swirling emotions aside and did what he always did when faced with a problem. He got practical.

Sitting in the wide bay window, he looked over at her. "Let's think about this. How long is she in for?"

"I don't know."

"What was she convicted of?" Same answer. "She's the one who left Parker with Child Services in the first place, right?"

"I don't know," Erin repeated through

clenched teeth. "They didn't offer that information, and frankly I didn't care. He was a kid who needed a loving home, and I wanted to be the one to give it to him."

She had stunningly few details about the boy she'd taken in, and Cam wasn't sure what to make of it. This wasn't a stray kitten or raccoon, which she'd rescued plenty of when they were kids. Parker was someone else's child, and apparently he'd come with a lot of baggage. Still, Cam couldn't help admiring her for what she was trying to do. It took a lot of courage to have a tender heart in such a tough world.

"Okay," he said, making up his response as he went along. "So she's been convicted of something bad enough to land her in prison. Based on what I've seen and heard, I think it's safe to assume that even if she didn't abuse Parker herself, she stood by while someone else did."

"That tracks with things he's told me."

Just thinking about what he must've been through made Cam's blood simmer. "Who could raise a hand against such a bright, friendly kid?"

"When he first came to live with me, he couldn't even look me in the eye. He only started calling me Erin a couple of weeks ago. It was the best Christmas present I ever got."

She added a smile that brought out the dimple in her left cheek. He remembered teasing her about it when they were younger, asking where she'd lost the right one. After a blistering glare, she'd smacked him in the chest and stalked away with her cute little nose in the air.

Where did that image come from? he wondered briefly before tucking it back into his small bank of good memories. The fact that a confrontation with her was there at all meant something, but right now he had other things that needed his attention.

"So," he continued in the tone he normally reserved for difficult subcontractors, "she doesn't have much of a leg to stand on if she wants to influence what happens to him."

"She's still his mother. Before I got into this, I asked the judge about her rights versus mine. He said that unless she legally signs away her parental interest, she can exercise it anytime she wants."

"I don't speak legalese," he grumbled. "What does that mean?"

"It means she can name another guardian to care for him until she's able to do it herself."

"Which could be years from now."

Erin shrugged. "That's the law."

"That's stupid."

"I know," she allowed with a slight grin, "but it's still the law. Even Parker insists she never hurt him. I take that to mean she just didn't keep the abuse from happening."

What kind of mother stands by and lets her kid suffer like that? Cam seethed silently. His own background wasn't the best, but he knew that if he and Natalie had been put in the line of fire that way, Mom would've taken them each by the hand and marched over to Granddad's house where they'd all be safe.

Grudgingly, he admitted that maybe Dad had done them all a favor by leaving before it came to that. It had torn their family apart, but at least no one had been physically harmed.

"Anyone who's spent five minutes with Parker can see that this is the best home he's ever had. If you need me to make some kind of statement or testify in court or something, let me know. I'll be there."

"Really?" A flicker of hope glimmered in her eyes, and she beamed at him like he was some kind of hero. "My family's offered to do that, and I love them for it. But it would carry more weight if it came from someone I'm not related to. Are you sure you want to get involved like that?"

"Absolutely." Seeking to lighten the intense moment, he grinned. "What are old enemies for?"

"We weren't enemies," she corrected him with a laugh. "We just didn't like each other."

"Y'know, I'm having a tough time remembering why."

He expected her to rattle off a list of his many faults or throw his most objectionable pranks in his face. To his amazement, she leaned in and kissed his cheek.

"That's funny. So am I."

Erin pulled back when she heard Parker's sneakers pounding down the creaky wooden steps. "He sounds like a baby elephant when he does that. Is it okay if I carpet those treads?"

"Sure," Cam replied easily, standing as Parker joined them by the window. Resting a hand on the boy's shoulder, he looked him in the eye as if he was an adult on his crew. "I think I've got an old remnant floating around in the cellar that we can use. Wanna learn how to lay carpet?"

"Yeah!"

Grabbing Cam's hand, he tugged their landlord toward the basement door while Erin called out, "No power tools!"

Cam waved his agreement, then snapped on

the lights before they disappeared down the narrow staircase.

Odd girl out, Erin thought. The story of her life. Eager to take a break from the chaos in their apartment, she put her hands on her hips and slowly spun, taking in the wide-open potential of the space that would soon house her store.

"My store," she murmured, savoring the way that sounded. She'd enjoyed working for the judge the past several years, and learning the ins and outs of family law had definitely served her well in navigating her challenging situation with Parker. But owning a business, being the one in charge, was something she'd always wanted.

Glancing up, she sent a little smile to her father. "I'm taking my shot, Dad. I hope you're proud of me."

A warm current swirled around her, and she couldn't help feeling as if he'd reached down from heaven to give her one of his famous bear hugs. He'd been gone four years now, ripped away from them in a car accident that had killed him instantly. Erin would give anything to see him one more time and have the chance to say goodbye.

But life didn't work that way, she reminded herself sternly, shrugging off the past as she decided what to do first. Since there wasn't much point in sweeping a floor that would soon be covered in ceiling tiles and sawdust, she opted for cleaning the grimy front windows.

It was a toss-up which was dirtier, the inside or the outside. It was a nice morning, so after she dug out her supplies she went out onto the sidewalk to get started. She hadn't been at it more than a minute when she heard her name being shouted from across the street. Turning, she saw Ellen Wheaton wave, then quickly check for traffic before hustling over to embrace her.

"Look at you," the pastor's wife crooned, beaming as if Erin had won a Nobel Prize. "Opening up your own business. How's it going?"

Laughing, Erin motioned to the tired-looking building. "What you see is what you get. How are your holidays going?"

"Crazy but wonderful. All six kids made it home for Christmas Day, and I'm taking a break from getting the house back to normal. I'm still not sure where we put twenty extra people, but somehow we made it work. How are you and Parker liking your new place?"

"Well, it's smaller than yours but it's pretty much destroyed, too, except for his room. He wasn't sure about the move, so I wanted him to feel comfortable right off the bat."

"Good for you," the motherly woman said, giving Erin's arm a pat of approval. "Kids don't stay young forever, so they have to come first."

She might not have Parker much longer, Erin worried with a frown. If she lost him just when he was beginning to make real headway, she wasn't certain she could bear it.

"Is something wrong, dear? You look pale all of a sudden."

"Oh, I'm fine. Just tired from all this unpacking." She felt awful not being truthful with the woman who'd stressed the importance of honesty in her Sunday school lessons, but Erin forced herself to smile. She didn't want to go around blurting out such a delicate problem and risk Parker hearing something that was sure to upset him. There was nothing either of them could do about it, so there was no point in dwelling on the negative.

"Oh, you poor thing. Before we settled here, we were reassigned to several churches, and all that moving was a lot of work." Something inside snared Ellen's attention, and she stared through the window as if she couldn't believe her eyes. "Is that Cam Stewart?"

"Yes. He's my new landlord and contractor,"

Erin explained, laughing at the sight of Parker trying to manhandle his end of the carpet roll.

Apparently it wasn't going well, because Cam said something and shouldered the runner himself. Ruffling Parker's hair, he motioned for his apprentice to go up the stairs ahead of him.

"How is Bridget doing?" Ellen asked.

"Cam said some days are better than others."

"Now that he's back in town, we'd love to see him on Sunday. Please let him know he's welcome to join us anytime."

Erin couldn't imagine why anyone would assume that she had any pull with the obstinate black sheep of the Stewart family. Beyond that, now that she knew he'd turned his back on God, there was no way she'd be mentioning church to him. "I'm sure he knows that already."

"I hope so. Well, I'd better be getting back to my own cleaning. Have a good morning."

"Thanks. You, too."

With another wave, Ellen went back the way she'd come, cheerful as a sunbeam in July. Erin's phone rang, and she pulled it out to check the caller ID, almost dreading what she might see. When her mother's picture came up, she let out a relieved sigh and answered. "Hi, Mom. How are you today?"

"Baking up a storm, getting stocked up for our New Year's Eve party."

"I thought I smelled something delicious." A long-standing event for the Kinleys, they hadn't thrown a New Year's party since Dad died. But this year, with both Mike and Drew getting married, their mother had decided it was time to reinstate the old tradition. And, true to form, she was doing it to the hilt.

"Aren't you sweet? How are you and Parker doing in town?"

"It's still a little chaotic, but we're fine." Glancing in the window, she watched while Cam held a yardstick and Parker drew a cut line the long way down the carpet remnant. "You won't believe who's been helping out today."

"Hmm, let me see. Your brothers are all busy clearing those limbs that came down in the front pasture the other day, so it's not one of them." She rattled off some more names, but after four, she laughed. "I give up. Who?"

"My landlord."

There was a long pause, and then her mother said, "Cam?"

"He hired Parker as his assistant, and they're putting carpet on those steps so it won't sound like a herd of elephants every time someone goes up or down."

"Well, isn't that nice of him?"

"Yeah. I didn't know he had it in him."

"You two have always been like oil and water," Mom lamented. "I never understood why you couldn't get along."

"We both like doing things our own way, and we don't compromise. Did you know he's divorced?"

"What a shame. I know he can be a challenge sometimes, but he's got such a good heart."

"I had no idea you thought of him that way," Erin confessed, intrigued by the gentle assessment of someone she'd always considered a thorn in her side.

"My friend Pauline's daughter is moving back here. I should introduce him to her."

"Don't bother," Erin advised, continuing her window cleaning while they chatted. "As soon as Bridget's on her feet again, Cam's going back to Minnesota."

"In the middle of winter?"

"I think he's nuts, too, but that's the plan. There's no cure for crazy."

Mom laughed, and Erin heard the whir of the commercial mixer they'd all chipped in to buy her for Christmas. "If you and Parker want a nice home-cooked meal tonight, come by the farm."

Her day hadn't started off all that well, and after her endless list of tasks was done, Erin could think of no better way to end it than in her mother's warm, family-filled kitchen. "That would be great. Thanks."

"Bring Cam along if he's free."

"Mom," Erin cautioned.

"To thank him for his help today," her mother added hastily. "Knowing him, he won't let you pay him for his time, so it's the least I can do."

"Are you sure that's the only reason?"

"Of course," she insisted stoutly. "I'm not one of those meddling, matchmaking kinds of people, you know."

"What about Mike and Lily?"

"They set themselves up when she was Abby's teacher. I just nudged."

"Uh-huh," Erin teased. "And then there's Drew and Bekah."

"The girl needed a place to stay, didn't she? So I donated a few things for her to use in that back room at the rescue center and set an extra place at the table once in a while."

Erin knew that tone, and she decided to play along. "But?"

"If you and Cam made peace and got to be friends, I wouldn't complain. Like you said, he's leaving eventually, so it would be nice if you two could bury that tired old hatchet before he goes. Life is short, honey, and the only one who gets hurt by a grudge is the one carrying it."

"That's one of Dad's," Erin commented, recognizing the slice of Irish wisdom immediately.

"That's how he lived his life, and I was always proud of him for it. I know it's not easy to forgive and forget, but in the end, it's best for everyone."

"I'll think about it," Erin hedged, although the concept didn't irk her the way it would have a few days ago. From agreeing to her terms on the building to befriending her shy foster son, Cam had surprised her several times since their awkward reunion. "I'll pass along your invitation, but don't be disappointed if he can't make it. At any rate, Parker and I will see you tonight at six. Can I bring anything?"

"Not a thing. See you then!"

Erin ended the call, smiling when a picture of her with Parker after the church Christmas pageant appeared on the screen. It was a real stretch sometimes, being his only parent, even though everyone in her family had generously taken the lost little boy into their hearts. She knew they'd had a tremendously positive impact on him.

But as she'd told Cam earlier, Parker should have a man in his life he could count on. Someone who would guide and teach him, who'd be patient when he needed a sympathetic ear but also urge him to realize his potential. His swift connection with the tall contractor amazed her, but it also made her sad.

Because Cam had made it clear that his stay in Oaks Crossing was temporary, and Parker needed someone who would be around for the long haul. That left him with Erin, and while she wasn't convinced that she was enough on her own, in her heart she knew one thing for certain.

She was better than nothing.

Chapter Four

By five that afternoon, Cam was beat.

Having worked construction for most of his adult life, he was used to long, demanding days and moving from one task to the next pretty much without a break. This project was something else again.

Parker was a quick study, eager to please and soaking in Cam's every word like a little sponge. He didn't touch anything he wasn't supposed to, and he was surprisingly helpful when Cam needed an extra pair of hands. The problem was Erin.

She had some very precise ideas about how to do...well, everything. Cam had anticipated that, and he took most of her directions in stride because he knew that if she approved of the final product, she'd be more likely to purchase the building when their three-month lease term ended.

And now, he was listening to her say for the hundredth time, "I think it would work better if we did it this way."

Finally at the end of his patience, he intentionally allowed some menace into his stare. "Do you?"

"Yes."

"Fine." Stepping away, he leaned back against his makeshift work bench and folded his arms. "Go ahead."

She blinked at him like a stunned owl, then shook her head. "I don't know how to actually *do* it."

"Just how it should be done. Right?" She glared at him, and he nudged Parker's shoulder with his elbow. "Girls."

He added a male wink, and the kid smiled. "Yeah. Abby can be pretty bossy sometimes, too."

"Whaddya do when she gets like that?"

The boy shrugged. "I let her have her way. She's younger, and besides I don't wanna make her mad."

"So," Cam commented, angling a look at his tormenter, "Mike's daughter inherited the famous Kinley temper. Imagine that."

"You two are hilarious," Erin shot back, but

the humor twinkling in her eyes let him know he'd made his point. "In my defense, this is going to be my store, and I'd like a say in how things are going to look."

"I can work with that," Cam agreed, glancing at his assistant. "How 'bout you?"

Erin had warned him that Parker was still timid about expressing his opinions to adults, so Cam expected him to simply nod. Instead, he flashed a mischievous grin. "Do I get paid the same?"

Cam laughed and held up his fist for a bump. "That's the way. Always get the terms up front, so you know what you're getting yourself into. And yes, you'll get paid the same no matter whose ideas we end up using."

"Okay."

"Now that we've settled our working arrangement," Erin interrupted, "it's getting late, and Grammy's expecting us at six. You should go get cleaned up for dinner."

"Yes, ma'am."

Parker scampered up the much quieter carpeted steps, leaving Cam alone with Erin for the first time since she'd taken her upsetting phone call from the social worker that morning. An awkward silence stretched out between them, even more noticeable considering the fact that they'd been poking at each other only a minute ago.

"Mom wanted me to invite you, too," Erin told him. "If you're not busy."

"Thank her for me, but I have to get home. I want to get in a shower before Mom's nurse leaves for the day."

"Another time, then."

"With everything I've got going, I doubt it." He winced at the pitiful edge on his voice and dredged up a half-hearted smile. "Sorry."

To his surprise, she reached a hand out and rubbed his shoulder. "It's tough running a business while you're caring for someone seven days a week. You need to make sure you take some time off, or you'll burn yourself out and be no good to anyone."

"I guess."

"Being here all day today probably didn't help."

"It was great," he blurted out before he had a chance to consider how it would come across to her. "The addition to the restaurant was a small job, and putting together a Laundromat doesn't take much imagination. This will be fun. As long as you stay outta my way," he added with a mock growl.

Her laughter brightened the rapidly darkening space. "Don't hold your breath. But I will promise to try not to step on those steel toes of yours if I can avoid it. Deal?"

She held out a small hand, and after a moment he accepted the gesture. "That'll work."

"Come on, now," she teased, flashing him a dimpled grin. "You've had more difficult clients than me."

Cam made a show of thinking that one over, then shook his head. "Nope."

She narrowed her eyes then tilted her nose in the air as she turned away. "Good. I like being number one."

The feisty comeback was just the kind of thing he expected from her, and he was still chuckling when he pulled the shop door closed behind him. It was a quick drive to his mother's house, and when he got there he frowned at the sight of yet another strange car parked in the driveway. Even more of a concern was the fact that the nurse was gone.

She knew how important it was for someone to be with Mom around the clock, Cam complained silently. What was going on? As soon as he opened the front door, he had his answer.

"You're kidding me!" a familiar downstate accent reached him in the foyer. "Then what did she do?"

"Chased him off with a frying pan," his mother's quieter, halting voice answered, and then he heard something that had become as rare as a blue moon these days. She laughed. "That bear never came back."

"Smart bear," her guest approved, looking up when Cam stopped in the archway. "Speaking of smart bears, how's my favorite godson?"

Strolling into the living room, Cam stooped to kiss her cheek. "I'm good, Aunt Connie. How're you?"

"Bored to death, with your uncle roaming the wilds of Tennessee on one of his boys' club hunting trips. So I decided to take a few days to go antiquing and come see my baby sister. I hope y'all don't mind me popping in this way without calling, but I'm too tired to drive another mile."

"Not a bit," he replied, noting the pink in Mom's cheeks and the lively sparkle in her eyes. "This is your home as much as ours, and you're welcome anytime."

"Good to have you," his mother added, beaming at her older sister affectionately.

Over her head, Cam mouthed, "Thank you."

His aunt gave him a quick wink and went on in her customarily brisk way. "I'm taking care of dinner tonight, to give Bridget a break from all that bachelor food."

"Hey, I'm a great cook," he protested, leaning against the door frame with a grin. "I can reheat meals from the café as well as anyone."

"Good boy," his mother said, gratitude shining in her eyes.

"Yeah, well, don't spread that around. I'm the black sheep of the family, remember?"

"Oh, you." Connie laughed, waving him off. "Get changed and go have some fun. We'll be girl-talking all night, and if you don't escape you'll be bored out of your skull."

"Can I talk to you first?"

The look she gave him made it obvious that she knew why he'd made the request. With a smile at her younger sister, she led him into the kitchen and turned to him with a calming gesture. "I know what you're going to say. I shouldn't have called Davey."

Cam hadn't heard the man referred to that way in years. It made him sound like a cuddly child's toy, and for some reason the nickname grated on nerves that had already been stretched to near their limits. "Then why did you?"

"He had a right to know what's been going on here," she whispered, sending a concerned look toward the living room. "They're still married, after all."

"A technicality," Cam retorted through grinding teeth. "Several times, Natalie and I tried to convince her to divorce him, but Mom's heart is too big for her own good. She still thinks there's hope for him."

"It's not your place to question your mother," Aunt Connie said, easing the scolding with an understanding smile. "You may be right, but circumstances are different now. She doesn't want any unfinished business when she—"

"Don't say it," he interrupted sternly. "She's not dying, so there's no need for her to be thinking that way. Unless someone she trusts put those thoughts into her head."

"Don't you be glowering at me like that, Cameron. I'd never do something like that to her, and you should be ashamed of yourself for even thinking I might. Bridget wants to make her peace on Earth so she can meet her Maker with a clear conscience."

"She didn't do anything to make him leave, so why does it matter?"

"Because it does. To her," his aunt added when he opened his mouth to argue further. "You don't share her faith, which is your choice. It's not right for you to deny her that comfort because you're angry at God."

This was one of those arguments he instinctively knew he couldn't win. *Never discuss politics or religion*, Granddad had cautioned him more than once. *You'll never change any-*

one's mind, and you'll alienate a lot of people while you're trying. So, in the interests of keeping things in his mother's house on an even keel, Cam decided to do something he seldom did. He backed down.

"All right," he conceded with a grimace. "You've got a point there."

"Of course I do," she replied, patting his arm proudly. "Now, you should pay attention to what I said and go have some fun. Working all day long and being cooped up here at night isn't good for someone your age."

"You make it sound like I'm still in high school."

"Oh, honey," Connie said, giving him a fond smile. "To me you'll always be the captain of the football team."

He wasn't sure what to make of that, but he decided not to waste any more time debating. Ten minutes later, he was freshly scrubbed and in his truck headed...

Where?

Cam hadn't had an evening to himself in so long, he wasn't sure what to do first. He was starving, but the only restaurant in town that served dinner was the Oaks Café, and he'd spent enough of his time there lately to last him the rest of his life. Rockville had a few nice spots, but after his challenging day, he wasn't in the mood to tackle the half-hour drive.

That left Maggie Kinley and the warm, welcoming kitchen where he'd felt at home for as long as he could remember. Her invitation to join the family tonight wasn't the worst offer he'd ever had, Cam mused as he turned onto the road that led to the outskirts of town and into the country.

As he left the streetlights behind him, he noticed a smattering of early stars strewn across the sky. They seemed to be dangling from nothing, accenting a full moon that glowed brightly over rolling hills of bluegrass and seemingly endless acres of old-growth oak trees that had given his hometown its name generations ago.

Out here, the houses were farther apart and ringed by huge expanses of farmland and white pasture fences that gave this part of Kentucky its unique charm. A couple of miles out, he found a freshly painted sign lit by a covered art-gallery-style bulb.

Gallimore Stables. Established 1910.

As he drove down the wide gravel lane it occurred to him that whenever he'd come here the Kinleys' horse farm had looked just the way it did now. That was a real accomplishment in a world that seemed to evolve into something new on a daily basis. All of Oaks Crossing shared the same commitment to tradition, he realized, and although he'd once considered that a negative, he was beginning to see the appeal of a place that had gracefully weathered the passage of time while keeping its character intact.

On either side of the driveway, long stretches of board fence framed pastures that led to dimly lit barns, where he knew a herd of many different breeds of horses was tucked in for the night. Some had been rescued from bad situations, while others had come from owners who couldn't keep them anymore. As their business, the Kinleys worked with retired racehorses, training them for use by new owners who wanted to ride the beautiful animals instead of race them.

Cam parked his truck in the turnaround beside a few other cars and smiled at the most inviting sight he could imagine on a day like this. Light spilled from all the windows of the rambling white farmhouse, adding to the festive Christmas lights outlining the roof and porch railings. When he reached the front door, he grinned as he reached into the opening of a huge wreath to press the button on a snowman's round stomach.

"Merry Christmas!" the thing yelled with a mechanical chuckle. "Come on in!"

Chuckling to himself, Cam opened the door and was met by the mouthwatering aromas of turkey, home-baked bread and cinnamon. Without looking left or right, he made a beeline for the kitchen and paused in the open doorway for another long whiff. "Wow, it smells amazing in here."

"Oh, it's not much, really. Just some leftovers from Christmas dinner," Maggie Kinley assured him in her usual offhand way.

Her apron directed him to Kiss the Cook, so he strolled in and did just that. "Best leftovers I've ever smelled. Thanks for inviting me."

"I had to, seeing as you haven't been here since Drew and Bekah's wedding," she chided him with a smile that reminded him of Erin's. "I can't figure out why you waited so long to come over and see us. You've always been welcome anytime."

"I've been kinda busy, with the restaurant and Mom and all." When Cam heard the whine in his voice, he cringed. "Sorry."

"For being honest? Please." She waved off his apology and reached up to pat his cheek. "We all have things to deal with, Cam, and these days you've got more than your share. Anytime you want to talk, you just come out here. I might not have an answer, but I can promise you I'll listen."

Made without any fanfare, her offer went a long way toward settling his riled-up nerves, and he had to admit that Erin could be right about him trying to manage everything on his own. "Thanks."

"Dinner will be a while longer, so have some cookies."

Glancing over to the long counter where containers of desserts were lined up like soldiers, he grinned. "I thought I smelled fresh snickerdoodles when I walked in. Did you make those for me?"

"And who else would I be making them for?" she demanded in a voice that still carried a tinge of Irish lilt.

"What would you have done if I'd decided to go to Rockville and catch a movie instead?" he asked as he took a small plate from the stack and piled on half a dozen cookies that were still warm from the oven and all but fell apart when he touched them.

"I'd just send them back into town with Erin, and she'd make sure you got them."

Cam wasn't used to having people want to take care of him, and while it wasn't a major deal, her sweet gesture touched him deeply. Maggie had sharp eyes, and she didn't miss much, so to conceal his sudden rush of emotion, he popped a snickerdoodle into his mouth.

"Oh, man," he groaned in appreciation. "I forgot how good these are."

"I'm glad you still like them. There's four dozen in the pantry for you to take home."

He felt like it was Christmas morning all over again. "Seriously?"

"Yes, but you have to share."

"There's always a catch," he grumbled, but he couldn't stop grinning. "Thanks, Maggie."

"You're welcome." Setting down her oven mitts, she poured him a tall glass of milk and set it on the oversize island for him. Then she pulled up a stool and rested her chin on her hands. "Now, tell me what's making you so angry."

"I'm not—" She tilted her head in a chiding gesture, and he sighed. "Okay, you got me."

And because you couldn't sit in Maggie's kitchen pounding down cookies and milk and not talk to her, he spilled his guts. He heard the usual bitterness and disgust, but other things he hadn't even realized he was feeling came pouring out. Things like hurt and regret, and a longing for how life had been when he was a child.

Before David Stewart had decided he didn't want a family anymore and walked away. The idea of opening up his family to that kind of heartache again made Cam so furious, he didn't know how to express it coherently.

When he was finished, it occurred to him that his head had slowly been drooping until he was staring down at the scarred butcher block under his empty plate. Out of sheer, stubborn pride he lifted his chin and looked at her. Maggie's eyes reflected the misery he'd grown up wrestling against, and for some reason, it made him feel slightly less pathetic.

"You need more cookies," she announced blithely, taking the plate to refill it. When she handed it back to him, she gave him a gentle, encouraging smile. "You know what you have to do."

"Yeah," he confided around a mouthful of cookie. "Doesn't mean I like it."

"This isn't about you, Cam. It's about what your mother wants—and needs—right now to ease her mind. Connie was right to call your father, but I agree that she should've warned you ahead of time. Does that help?"

Not really, but she'd been so patient and understanding, he didn't have the heart to tell her so. "A little, I guess. Thanks for listening."

"Remember, you don't have to forgive him. You just have to tolerate him."

Cam gave her a long, suspicious look. "That doesn't sound like you."

"Forgiveness isn't easy, especially when the hurt runs so deep. It might not even be possible for you, at least, not yet. I raised four hardheaded children, and if I've learned anything, it's that you can't convince someone to do something they're not ready for."

"A thousand years might do it," he joked with a wry grin. "Then again, maybe not."

"I vote for not," a sarcastic voice chimed in from behind him, and he turned to find Erin coming through the doorway. Settling on the stool beside him, she added, "I'm surprised to see you here. Whatever you're talking about, you're too stubborn to give in. That's one thing I always liked about you."

"Seeing as Kinleys are genetically obstinate on both sides," he fired back, winking at Maggie.

"You Scots are no more tractable than we Irish are," Maggie assured him as she headed toward the pantry. "You just roll your words differently."

When she was gone, he turned to Erin. "Well, she's got a point there. You could argue with my great-uncle Magnus forever and hardly understand a word he was saying."

"Good strategy on his part. That way, he was never wrong."

They both laughed, and he nudged the plate toward her. "Cookie?"

"Sure." She didn't inhale it the way he had, and in between nibbles she asked, "Feeling better?"

"Some. I forgot how easy your mom is to talk to."

"She's pretty much heard it all, so she's a good sounding board. I saw your expression when I walked in here, and I'm guessing you didn't like hearing what she had to say." Cam nutshelled their conversation for her, and she nodded solemnly. "I wouldn't like it much, either, but she's right, about doing it for your mother. If it's that important to her, you have to make it happen."

Something in her tone caught his attention, and he took a shot. "Is that what she told you about meeting Parker's mom?"

"Yeah," Erin grumbled while she filled an empty glass with milk. "Parker's situation is dicey enough as it is, and if I can get on this woman's good side by caving in to what she wants, that's what I have to do. Sometimes being a grown-up is the worst."

"I'll drink to that."

They clinked glasses in a morose toast over

a childhood snack, and it dawned on him that he'd just shared a pleasant, no-strings-attached moment with Erin Kinley. Stranger things had happened to him, he supposed, but at the moment he couldn't think of any.

"Y'know," he heard himself saying, "I could go with you if you want."

"Why would you offer? It doesn't sound like a fun day for you."

"Well, I assume your mom was planning to go along for moral support, but it'd be easier for me than for someone who's never been there."

Erin's eyes nearly bugged out of her head, and her mouth dropped into a shocked O. "Who did you know in prison?"

"An old girlfriend in Ohio. Long time ago," he added just to be clear. Then, because he couldn't resist yanking Erin's chain, he said, "She wanted me to water her plants for three to five years."

"You're hopeless," she hissed, shaking her head in a maternal gesture he assumed she'd picked up from Maggie. "Did you really go?"

"Like I'd lie about visiting someone in prison. It was only once, but I know the drill, so the security and rules won't freak me out. If you want some company, I don't mind going with you."

It struck him as being an odd thing to say, and judging by the flabbergasted look on Erin's face, she thought so, too. But then a grateful smile replaced the shock, assuring him that his crazy proposition had been worth the risk.

"That would be great, Cam. I know Mom will really appreciate not having to do that."

"For the woman who still makes me my favorite cookies? No problem."

Actually, he would've done it for Erin, no perks needed. But since he still wasn't sure why, he decided to keep the comment to himself.

Scrounging around in a cupboard, Erin found some wheat crackers and a wax-coated wedge of unpronounceable cheese in the selection one of her aunts had sent them for the holidays. While she and Cam dug in to their snack, she casually mentioned, "I've been thinking about the design for Pampered Paws."

"Aw, man," he groaned, although his dark eyes twinkled in fun. "I know that look. Whenever you start thinking, it always means more work for me."

Her first impulse was to stick her tongue out at him, but she managed to stop herself. He'd been incredibly helpful already, and hadn't asked her for anything except to pay for the materials. But she couldn't keep all that annoyance in, so she settled for rolling her eyes. "Don't be so dramatic. I'm perfectly willing to give you a hand."

"You say that like it's a good thing."

"Anyway," she spit out through a totally fake smile, "I was thinking it'd be nice to have a spot where people can play with some animals. I don't want to house live animals at the store, but we can bring in puppies and kittens from the rescue center once in a while so folks can see them and maybe take a few home when they leave."

Still munching, he hummed in a way that she took to mean something like "interesting." After swallowing, he said, "That could work. You could even make it a promotional event that lures folks into the store to see what's new."

"I like that idea," she approved, dipping a cracker into a tin labeled Hummus for the Holidays.

"Yeah, I get 'em once in a while."

She didn't doubt that in the slightest, but she'd never tell him so. He'd go back to being intolerable again, and then she'd be hardpressed not to strangle him. "What else have you got?"

He started to answer but a sleek black helicopter floated through the wide doorway to hover over the breakfast bar. Over the speaker, she heard Parker's voice. "Requesting cookie load for search and rescue crew. Over."

"Josh got him that thing for Christmas," Erin explained as she went to fill the order. "He's been having a blast playing chopper pilot."

"Josh or Parker?"

Laughing, she replied, "Both."

Just as she was about to drop some cookies into the toy's payload basket, Cam stopped her with a mischievous grin. "Base to Chopper One. Please clarify type of cookie required. Over."

"Oatmeal. Over."

Cam gave Erin a quizzical look, and she realized that his question was aimed at trying to find out who was in charge of the remote control. Grinning, she shook her head and murmured, "Parker likes chocolate chip."

"Chopper One," he barked in a commanding tone. "Have you been hijacked?"

There was a pause, then a chuckle that was much too deep to be her son. "Cam, what're you doing in there?"

"Guarding the cookie supply. If you ask for snickerdoodles, we're gonna have a problem."

Now that she knew the real story, Erin added

cookies for Parker and Abby and announced, "Payload complete. Back to the sky with you."

"You're supposed to say 'over,' Aunt Erin," her niece politely reminded her.

"If Grammy finds out you've been sneaking cookies right before dinner, it'll all be over."

"Roger that," Josh broke in, and the copter banked into a neat turn and headed back to the living room.

After peace had been restored, Cam sat back in his seat and folded his arms in a classic I'm-listening pose. "Go ahead."

It took Erin a minute to get back into designing mode, but by the time dinner was ready, they'd sketched out how to best use the enormous space she had available for her store.

"You're really good at this," she complimented him while she helped ferry hot dishes over to the always-crowded table.

"Everyone's got a knack for something," he replied with a shrug. "I guess building stuff is mine."

He seemed uncomfortable with her praise, which was the last thing she'd have expected from him. The guy she recalled so vividly had been confident to the point of arrogance, and he'd never given her the impression that he had an ounce of humility. Then again, they were older now, and he'd been through a lot recently. Sad as his mother's condition obviously was for him, maybe coping with it had the unexpected benefit of bringing him down to earth a little.

When all nine Kinleys were around the old oak table, Erin took a moment to drink in the sight of the people she loved more than anything in the world. As head of the family, Mike sat in the "dad" chair now. At the foot, Maggie began filling plates and passing them around while three different conversations continued from wherever they'd left off in the other room. The one that interested Erin most was about the big shindig planned for New Year's Eve, and she turned to Parker.

"This is your first New Year's here with us. Any requests?"

He considered that for a few seconds and then his eyes lit up. "I've heard about the ball that drops in New York City, but I've never seen it. Can we watch it on TV?"

"You think you can stay awake that long?"

"Sure. Jamie and Dennis are my age, and they're going to."

Kid logic, she thought with a grin. You had to love it. She vaguely remembered being that way, before life had taught her that things didn't always turn out the way you want them to. Fathers died suddenly, boyfriends decided they'd rather be with someone else. Little boys with troubled blue eyes melted your heart and made you want to wrap your arms around them so no one could ever hurt them again.

It must be the time of year, Erin thought as she blinked away a rare rush of tears. The sentimentality surrounding the holidays had the tendency to make her think too much about everything.

Something brushed her leg, and she glanced down to see Abby's golden retriever, Charlie, pawing at her knee, a woebegone look on his furry face. Behind him was Mike's old terrier Sarge, sitting at a polite distance but with the same begging look in his eyes. Making sure Mom was engrossed in the discussion about the leaky attic roof, Erin sneaked a piece of turkey to each of the dogs.

"Softie," Cam teased, nudging her shoulder with a grin.

"I can't help it," she murmured back. "They look so pitiful."

"The kids've been feeding them over here, so they're hardly starving. Those hounds have you pegged but good."

"What can I say? I love animals."

He glanced around her to the smug-looking dogs. "From the looks of it, they love you back. Speaking of which, Bekah was talking about your new residents at the rescue center earlier. How're things going over there?"

In reply, Erin held up her hand and rocked it. "We squeaked through last year, but we have some new funding starting up January first. I'm really hoping we can attract a full-fledged veterinarian to come and stay for a while. Our last one was a fill-in, and with our shoestring budget, we couldn't pay him enough money to become permanent."

"Can't you use a vet from around the area?"

Frowning, she shook her head. "We need an all-rounder who can manage pets and a variety of wildlife. Someone like that isn't easy to find for the salary we're offering. Most vets have staggering college loans, so they have to make enough to cover those payments and then have some kind of life besides."

"Hey, Erin." Her little brother Josh, who towered over her, leaned forward to get her attention from the other end of the bench. "I was talking to the clerk at the farm store today, and he said he knows someone who just graduated from veterinary school and might be interested in coming here."

Her heart jumped at the news, and then cold, hard reason swept in to blow her excitement away. "Coming here or staying here?"

"He didn't say."

"Did you maybe think to get a name?" She loved him to pieces, but he was the least organized person she'd ever known. How he could be familiar with every inch of ground on the farm but be totally clueless about important details like names was beyond her.

"Shore did." Grinning, he held his hand out to show her some faded scribbling on his palm. "Aren't ya proud of me?"

"I'd be prouder if you'd put it in your phone and could text it to me." The grin widened, and she shook her head at him. "You lost another one, didn't you?"

"Yeah. That's why I get those super-cheap models. They always fall outta my pocket when I'm working and I don't realize they're gone till someone like you hassles me about typing stuff into my phone."

"Whatever." Taking out her own sleek cell, she snapped a picture of his hand and squinted at the result. The name was more or less illegible, but thankfully the number was clearer. "I can't read any of these letters."

Consulting his hand, he said, "Heather Fitzgerald."

"A woman," Bekah commented from her seat next to Drew. "Sierra and I were saying not long ago how great it would be if we could hire a female vet."

"Definitely," Lily chimed in with a smile down at her stepdaughter. "Girls can do anything boys can do, right, Abby?"

Big brother Mike glowered his opinion of that. "Will someone please tell me when this place turned into a beauty parlor?"

"The day you brought Lily home," Erin retorted.

"Actually, she followed me here. I tried everything I knew to get her to leave."

"Actually," Lily echoed him sweetly, "I just wanted riding lessons. The rest was your idea."

"You really liked her, Daddy," Abby reminded him. "That's why she kept coming back."

Cam laughed, grinning across the table at Bekah. "Is that your story, too?"

"Not exactly."

Hugging Drew's arm, she gave him a smile filled with gratitude. She didn't say anything more, but from where Erin was sitting, words couldn't have done her expression justice. Somehow, her goofy older brother had found the one woman on the planet able to see through his overgrown kid routine to his generous heart and love him just the way he was.

Seeing two of her brothers so happily married was wonderful, and she wished them nothing but the best with their wives. Still, there was a tiny part of her that couldn't help being envious of the joy and contentment they'd found. Wanted it for herself, even though she had to admit she didn't have the slightest idea about how to go about getting it.

Then again, she reminded herself, a brand-new year was right around the corner, full of possibilities and potential. As an adult, putting the old year behind her and starting with a clean slate had become one of her favorite things about the holidays. No matter what had gone wrong during the past twelve months, she liked knowing that the future could be anything she wanted.

She just had to figure out how to make it happen.

Chapter Five

Two nights later, Erin was back in her mother's kitchen refilling a tray with pigs in a blanket when she heard a knock on the back door. Framed in the Christmas lights was Cam, who held up a hand in greeting. She couldn't imagine why he hadn't come in the front like everyone else, so she wiped cooking spray off her hands with a towel and opened the door. "What are you doing out here?"

"Nice greeting. You get many visitors?"

"Sorry. I was surprised to see you skulking around back there, is all."

"I'm not skulking," he corrected her as he closed the door behind him. "I'm avoiding. Did your mom invite the entire population of Oaks Crossing?"

"Pretty much. It's the first New Year's party

she's thrown since Dad died, so she wanted to do it up right."

"Go big or don't bother," he added with a grin. "That's the Kinley way."

He settled on a stool and broke off a small bunch of grapes before popping one in his mouth. While she picked up where she'd left off rolling hot dogs in dough, she casually asked, "So, how did things go for you yesterday?"

"Fine," he replied in between bites. "Nothing broke, and I got started on the year-end bookkeeping and inventory."

"That's good, right?" By the glower she received in reply, she assumed she'd gotten that one wrong. Frustrated by his insistence on seeing the gloomy side of everything, she flattened her palms on the island and nailed him with her best mom look. "Cam, you have to stop being such a grouch. It's bad for you and everyone who has to deal with you."

"Meaning you?"

"Well, yes, if you want to know the truth. Why don't you at least try looking on the bright side for a change? Who knows? You might even like it," she added with a little grin.

"You mean, like a New Year's resolution?" She nodded, which only made him frown. "I've never been into those. Most folks end up ditching whatever new habit they promised to make, and then they feel guilty about it."

"I have no doubt that if you put your mind to it, you could improve your outlook. I'm not talking blinding rays of sunshine here. More like something in the tan range."

"What makes you think I can even manage that?"

Although he was still arguing with her, she detected a slight twinkle in his dark eyes that told her she'd snared his attention, if not his agreement. "You have a fabulous sense of humor, even if it is a tad sarcastic. That means you know when something's funny, and you can appreciate the humor in a situation. Just listen to that part of you more often, and you'll be much happier."

"And so will the people who have to deal with me," he said, echoing her earlier comment.

"Exactly."

Popping the last grape into his mouth, he picked up two of the plastic stem glasses she'd filled with ginger ale for guests. Handing one to her, he held his in the air. "Here's to new perspectives and a year full of good things to come."

"I'll drink to that."

They tapped glasses to seal the toast, and

Erin sipped the bubbles while Cam downed his in one gulp.

"Great vintage, but not much kick," he joked. "Last year, I celebrated New Year's in Vegas with my buddies."

She hated to consider what kind of mischief they'd been up to. "I've heard that's a crazy place all year long. I can only imagine what they do for New Year's."

"Whatever you've seen on TV, it's ten times bigger and brighter. It's fun but not something I'd share with my family, if you know what I mean."

What a life he'd had since leaving their tiny hometown, she thought with more than a smidgen of envy. While she cherished being close to her family, she had to admit she wouldn't mind having a chance to spread her wings just a little, to see what they could do.

But at her age, with a child depending on her, she'd have to settle for something a bit more doable, like opening a pet store. That would be an adventure, too, and she wouldn't have to leave the ground to make it happen. Quite honestly, she wasn't sure if she considered that a plus or a minus.

"So, what's your resolution for next year?"

Cam's voice pulled her from her brooding, and she gladly focused on something more concrete. "To adopt Parker and make Pampered Paws a raging success."

"I'm no expert, but those sound like goals, not new behavior. What else've you got?"

His opinion rankled at first, but after a few seconds, she recognized that he had a point. She tended to be very task-oriented, believing that if she did X, Y would happen. Although she acknowledged that she was far from perfect, she'd never really thought much about how to be a better person.

"I'm not sure." Inspiration struck, and she decided to risk asking him for advice. "What do you think I should improve?"

To her surprise, he laughed. "Not a chance. I've been married, and that's a troublemaker question if ever I heard one."

"Oh, come on. You must've noticed something these past few days. Just be honest, but nice," she cautioned, pointing at him for emphasis. "I promise not to take it wrong."

Leaning back in his chair, he folded his arms and studied her for a long, uncomfortable few moments. Erin felt like a bug squirming under a magnifying glass, and she fought the urge to take back her request.

"Okay, but you asked." Pausing, he went on in a somber tone. "I think you take things too seriously."

"I have a lot of responsibilities, you know," he chided her with a tilt of his head, and she couldn't help laughing at herself for proving him right so quickly. After all, she'd just told him to be more positive about his situation, so she had to be willing to take some criticism in return. "Okay, you got me there. It's true."

Leaning forward, he rested his arms on the counter and folded his hands in an earnest pose that in her mind didn't fit his cocky personality at all. "With the rescue center, your new business and being a single mom, you've got a lot to manage. You do it all really well, but you have to remember you're still Erin, and she needs to breathe once in a while."

"You sound like you know that from personal experience."

"Yeah," he admitted on a heavy sigh. "For the past ten years, all I did was breathe. It was fun, but—" He shrugged as if he couldn't find the words to express what he meant.

"It was lonely," she filled in the blank for him, adding a sympathetic smile. "Even though you got to spend New Year's at a casino with your bachelor friends."

"Yeah." Glancing through the hallway into the crowded living room, he came back to her with a wry grin. "Don't tell anyone, but I actually like this a lot better."

"Don't worry," she assured him with a wink. "Your secret's safe with me."

When they reached the dining room, Erin paused to assess what they had enough of and what needed replenishing. The old buffet on the side wall held two spiral hams, a platter of roast beef and whole chickens so big they could have passed for turkeys. Alongside the meats were bowls of different gravies, baskets of rolls and four different kinds of salad for anyone who'd made a diet part of their plan for the coming year.

There was an entire table of finger foods for the kids, which was where she and Cam set their blanketed pigs and chicken fingers. The tater tots were running low, and she made a mental note to pop some more into the oven. The desserts were holding up well, but that was probably because folks hadn't finished their meals yet.

Cam let out a low whistle of appreciation. "Maggie really outdid herself in here. How are we ever gonna eat all this food?"

"Oh, you know Mom," Erin replied as she straightened up some cockeyed platters and bowls. "She makes way too much, then shuttles the leftovers to folks all over town. Including us."

"Did you know that if you nuke snickerdoodles in the microwave long enough, they smell like freshly baked cookies? Taste like 'em, too."

He added a boyish grin totally at odds with his tall, dark and dangerous appearance, and she was struck by how much more at ease he seemed than when he'd arrived. Apparently, her impromptu scolding had done Cam some good.

"Five minutes to midnight!" Josh hollered, hanging on the door frame as he leaned into the dining room. "Y'all better grab someone to kiss, 'cause the ball's about to drop."

Before she could chide him for being an idiot, he was gone. When she turned to Cam to apologize, she found him studying her intently. "What?"

"Just wondering who you kissed last year."

"Funny," she shot back, sidling past him, "I was wondering the same thing about you."

Chuckling, he followed her into the living room where about a hundred guests were clustered around the humongous-screen TV Lily had bought Mike for Christmas. The expansive view of Times Square was incredible, and Erin heard the announcer saying there were over a million people crammed into the theater district of Manhattan. Even more hung out of windows, bundled up against the cold while they gazed up at the ball covered in crystals and lights.

Cam took two glasses of ginger ale from a nearby table and offered her one. Normally, she enjoyed New Year's, but for some reason, this one felt very awkward to her. As if sensing her discomfort, he leaned in and murmured, "Don't look so panicked, bug. I'm not gonna kiss you."

"Thanks."

"Unless you want me to," he amended with a shameless grin.

Shaking her head, she muttered, "Does that usually work for you?"

"What?"

"The charming scoundrel routine. The women up north must fall all over you when you look at them like that."

"Like what?"

"Oh, don't play dumb with me," she retorted, laughing in spite of herself. "You know exactly what you're doing, and I'm not buying it. I've known you too long to fall for that."

"Can't blame a guy for trying," he said, grinning at her as if he couldn't care less that she didn't want to share the traditional midnight kiss with him. Or anyone else, for that matter. She'd had her fill of being someone else's plus one, and was more than happy to finally be doing things her own way.

Most of the time, anyway. Thankfully, Parker came over to join them, and she put her grown-up problems away for later. Cam handed him a stemmed glass of ginger ale, and he stared up at his new friend with hero worship in his eyes. "Thanks."

"No problem. What've you got in mind for the New Year?"

"I'm gonna win the ten-and-under division of the Bluegrass Science Fair," her foster son replied immediately.

"Yeah? What're you planning to build?"

"I haven't decided yet," Parker confided soberly, "but when I do, I'm gonna make sure it's the best project there."

"I'd like to see that."

Parker's face lit up the way it had the first time the two of them had bonded over their shared love for Cam's old truck. "Could you come? That would be so cool!"

"Just let me know when and where. I'll be there."

Erin's trouble radar started pinging, but she didn't want to spoil their moment. Parker had been disappointed and outright mistreated by so many of the adults he'd known, she was adamant that anyone who made a promise to him had to be beyond certain that they were capable of keeping it. While she didn't doubt that Cam meant to attend the regional event, she wasn't at all convinced that he would end up coming.

The concern she felt must have showed on her face, because Cam leaned toward her to murmur, "I'll be there, Erin. I promise."

Dad had always said a man's true intentions showed in his eyes, and when she looked up into Cam's she saw nothing but quiet confidence. Then, as if her attention had knocked something loose, another emotion drifted in to twinkle in the dark depths. She knew she should break the unexpected connection with him, but she couldn't make herself look away.

While they stood there staring at each other, she was vaguely aware of everyone else in the room counting down the final ten seconds.

"Happy New Year!" everyone shouted, cheering and toasting to mark the occasion.

"I did it, Erin," Parker crowed proudly, giving her a quick hug. "I stayed up until midnight."

"You sure did, honey. Good for you."

Flashing her a delighted smile, he bolted away with Abby and several young cousins, making a beeline for the dessert table in the hallway.

True to his word, Cam didn't kiss her, not

even on the cheek. Instead, he tapped her glass with his and smiled. "Happy New Year, bug."

"You know," she informed him primly, "you're the only one who calls me that anymore."

"Well, you know me. I'm partial to the classics."

"Whatever. Happy New Year to you, too," she relented with a smile of her own. "I hope it turns out the way you want."

"Back atcha."

After downing his drink, he gave her a cocky grin and sauntered off to mingle with the other guests. Erin watched him go, admiring the confident way he moved through the crowd, shaking hands and trading small talk as if he was in the dining room at the Oaks Café. She'd always considered him kind of detached by nature, and she was impressed by this new side of her childhood tormenter.

When she realized she was staring after him, she jerked herself back to reality and started collecting empty plates and cups for the trash. In the kitchen, she ran into Bekah, who'd stepped in and taken over replenishing the buffet without even being asked.

"What a party," she approved, pulling out the tater tots Erin had shoved into the oven earlier. "I didn't think it was possible to top

Christmas, but you guys really know how to celebrate the holidays." As proof, she tugged on the waistband of her jeans.

"Oh, stop," Erin chided with a laugh. "You're the tiniest one in the family besides the kids."

Bekah grinned back, and there was something in her expression that caught Erin's attention. A gleam in Bekah's eyes that said she had a secret and wasn't opposed to sharing it. Suddenly it hit her, and Erin gasped. "No."

"Yes," Bekah responded, giggling a bit. "We found out today, and the doctor said to keep it to ourselves for a while. But I'm so jazzed, I just had to tell someone."

Erin was pretty jazzed herself, and she circled around the breakfast bar to embrace her. "Does Mom know?"

Bekah nodded. "But that's it. Please don't tell anyone."

"Never. And I promise to act surprised when you and Drew make your big announcement."

"Thanks."

"Thank you for trusting me," Erin said humbly. "I know that's not easy for you."

"I'm getting better at it, thanks to your family and everyone in there." Bekah nodded toward the raucous crowd milling around the farmhouse's large first floor. "This time last year, I was living in a closet-sized room over a twenty-four-hour Thai restaurant, and now I have a wonderful life with Drew and more to come. What a difference a few months make."

"I know what you mean. Last year, I'd just broken off the worst relationship ever and had the wild idea to start my own business. When I took on Parker in the middle of all that, it seemed even crazier, but it's turned out to be the best decision I could've made."

"It makes you think, doesn't it? I mean, what would've happened if you'd gone left instead of right? You'd end up in a whole other place, and everything would be different, especially for Parker." Looking over, she added a warm smile. "You saved that sweet little boy from a very uncertain future, Erin. You gave him a safe, stable home and this big family to love him. You couldn't have given him a better gift if you'd tried."

"You're sounding like a mom already," Erin teased with a fond smile. "But thanks for saying it, anyway. It's nice to hear."

"Anytime you need some perspective, ask me. I've been through the ringer, and I thank God every day for sending me here. I don't know what would've happened to me otherwise."

It wasn't like Bekah to be so forthcoming about herself, and Erin suspected that Drew's steady, constant love had a lot to do with her newest sister-in-law opening up to her this way. Bekah picked up a large basket of rolls and carried it into the dining room, leaving Erin alone for the first time all day. The bit of solitude gave her time to reflect on the year that had gone by and the one that had just begun.

While she pondered everything that had changed for her recently, she was surprised to discover that Cam headed the list. Not as her landlord, but as an unexpected friend and champion, supporting her in her new venture and the unpleasant task of somehow coming to terms with Lynn Smith.

Unappealing as it was, Erin realized that once she cleared that hurdle, the path to adopting Parker should be easier to navigate. She still had dozens of legal hoops to go through, and she suspected that by the time she was finished, she'd feel like a trained dolphin being put through its paces.

But a forever home with her was what Parker prayed for every night before she tucked him into bed. And no matter what it took, she'd do everything in her power to make sure his prayer was answered.

The following morning, Cam tried to sleep in the way his aunt had ordered him to. But after staring at the ceiling for a while, he got bored listening to the cornball morning show on his old clock radio and got ready to face what promised to be another long, tiring day. Oddly enough, he thought while he finished shaving, he didn't feel as dragged out as he had the morning before.

Apparently, the Kinley farm hadn't lost any of its charm for him. Since he was a kid, whenever he'd gone there, he'd come back feeling a lot better about whatever had been bothering him when he'd arrived. And since he'd reluctantly become the man of his family when he was only twelve, there had always been plenty going on for him to be upset about.

Determined not to let his mood take such a gloomy turn, he shook off the pessimism that had become a part of his daily routine lately and forced himself to focus on the good things that had been happening. Aunt Connie being here was a big plus, especially since her visit seemed to be making Mom feel better than all the medicine in the world. Thanks to the upgrades he'd made, the Oaks Café was holding its own in a tough economy. And the building that had been nothing more than an aggravating cash drain was finally generating some much-needed income.

When he considered all that, he could almost

stand to think about the impending meeting
with his father.

The face staring back at him darkened with
an expression that would've made anyone hesi-
tant about approaching him. Shaking his head,
Cam wiped the steamy mirror and turned off
the bathroom light. While he'd love to put this
off until his father got tired of waiting and
went back to Michigan, he knew it was best to
quit stalling and get it over with. Mom wanted
to see her husband, and while the idea twisted
Cam's gut into knots, he didn't have the heart
to deny her something that seemed to be so
important to her.

The house was still quiet, so he sneaked out
the front door to his car, opening and closing
his driver's door as softly as he could. Holding to his decision to get the unpleasant task
over with, he dialed the number on the business card and waited. He half expected to be
shuffled to voice mail, but his father answered
on the second ring.

"This is David Stewart," he said in a brisk,
businesslike tone.

"It's Cam. If you still want to meet, today's
good for me."

"How about lunch here in Rockville?" his
father suggested without hesitation. "My treat."

Cam had anticipated that the man would

insist on meeting in Oaks Crossing, and he had to admit that he appreciated the suggestion to connect on more neutral ground. "Fine. I'll be at the Farmer's Grill at noon."

"So will I. And Cam?"

"Yeah?"

There was a slight pause before he went on. "I know this can't be easy for you, and I'm grateful to you for giving me another chance."

"I'm giving you the chance to buy me lunch and talk. If I don't like what you have to say, I'm outta there."

"Fair enough. I'll see you at noon."

Already stretched beyond his limited patience, Cam hung up without saying anything more. All the way to the restaurant, he questioned the wisdom of agreeing to see someone who got his hackles up just by breathing the same air. But it was done now, and he had no choice but to see it through. Part of him was confident that his father hadn't changed a bit, and this encounter would turn out to be a pointless waste of time.

Another part, the one that was still a heartbroken boy watching out the window for his dad to come home, hoped that, somehow, things would end differently than they had back then.

Since he had no control over either outcome,

Cam settled for dropping by the café to make sure breakfast was running smoothly. The dining room was humming with the usual early morning activity, and he stopped to chat with several customers on his way into the kitchen. Braced for another catastrophe, he was relieved to find that the crew seemed to be busy but managing well.

As if that weren't enough, Kyle grinned at him from the open grill. "Walk-in cooler's running like a champ. We just finished putting away the food delivery about ten minutes ago."

"You're kidding me." When the kid shook his head, Cam couldn't deny being pleased. "That's great. I guess you don't need me, then."

"Not till three. The new meat guy's making his rounds and is coming by to meet you."

"Schmooze me, you mean. Since it's a new year, I imagine he'll be bringing us some good stuff."

"You wouldn't want to share with your employees, would you?" he asked, flipping a series of pancakes in a practiced motion.

"A definite possibility," Cam replied, feeling generous. "We'll see what he's got, then go from there."

"Sounds good. Will you be next door again today?"

"Mostly." He tucked several fresh Danish

into a white takeout bag imprinted with the Oaks Café logo and filled two to-go cups with coffee. Taking them in one hand, he opened the side door with the other. "Call my cell if you need me."

"Will do."

Kyle stacked the pancakes on a plate and dinged the pick-up bell with his spatula. As he left the bustling kitchen, Cam recalled doing that himself about a million times. No better way to learn the family business, Granddad had insisted, than from the ground up.

More than once, Cam had wished that the old man was still around to see what he'd accomplished in the past few months. Although he wasn't one to dwell on images of the hereafter, he liked to picture his grandfather in heaven, smiling with pride. Right before telling him to quit mooning around and get back to work.

In front of the soon-to-be pet store, Cam was fishing out his keys when the door swung open. Clearly dressed for hard labor, Erin gave him a curious look. "Is something funny?"

"No. Why?"

"You were grinning just now."

"Just remembering someone."

"Oh." Stepping back, she let him walk through. "Anyone I know?"

He knew that fake-careless tone well, and he couldn't keep back a chuckle. "Not a girl, if that's what you're after."

"I'm not after anything," she informed him airily. "Just making conversation."

"Uh-huh. So where's my apprentice?"

"Dead asleep upstairs. While we have some time, I was thinking you and I could block out those designs we settled on last night and make a list of what we need."

"Funny," he said, showing her the bag he'd brought with him. "I was thinking we'd start with breakfast."

"I already ate."

Her clipped tone alerted him to some kind of trouble in Erin-land, and in light of their conversation the night before, he was instantly concerned. When she didn't offer any kind of explanation, he decided she didn't feel like sharing whatever it was. He thought he'd done a pretty fair job as a sounding board, so her reluctance to confide in him now bothered him. Then again, despite having grown up with his mother and younger sister, women were notoriously difficult for him to understand. If anyone doubted that for even a second, they could ask his ex-wife.

Hoping to draw her out with some well-placed sarcasm, he said, "Then I guess that leaves more for me."

He set her coffee on the work bench and strolled down to the other end. Pulling up one of the stools, he made a decent show of ignoring her. The trouble with that was, he couldn't quite keep his eyes off her.

The skinny tomboy he'd spent his teenage years harassing had matured into a more feminine version of her brothers, slender but strong. Her light brown hair was pulled up in a ponytail that fell down her back in waves that made him think of honey. While she sipped her coffee and flipped through their rough sketches making notes, he couldn't help noticing the snap of intelligence in her eyes.

Unfortunately, there was a hint of desperation there, too, as if she was forcing herself to concentrate on something besides whatever was bothering her. Cam could relate to that, and after several minutes, he decided he couldn't just sit there and watch her struggle without at least trying to help her.

"Erin."

She didn't even glance his way. "What?"

"Look at me."

"Why?"

The woman would try the patience of a man far more tolerant than he. Rather than repeat himself and have her continue to give him the cold shoulder, he got up and walked down to stand in front of her. When that didn't work, he went down on his knee in the sawdust and looked up at her. "Tell me what's wrong."

The eyes that met his flooded with a disturbing combination of anger and fear, but she quickly masked it with the flinty look he'd gotten from her more times than he cared to recall. "Haven't you got enough problems of your own?"

"I think I can manage one more." The urge to take her in his arms and comfort her was almost overwhelming. To avoid the temptation, he pulled away to a more respectable distance. Sitting on the floor, he stretched his legs out in front of him and leaned back on his hands. "Try me."

"I talked to Parker's social worker, Alice, this morning. She said the agency is concerned about me losing my job."

"The judge retired. That's not the same as getting fired. And you've got that severance he paid you."

"It's not a steady income, and she said that while she knows I have plenty of support here, my current situation doesn't look good on paper. If she can't convince the committee otherwise, they can actually declare me a bad risk and put him back into the foster system."

Her miserable tone said more than any words possibly could. Fortunately for Cam, she wasn't the weepy type. He wasn't sure he could keep it together if this intelligent, strong-willed woman started to cry. "So, you need a job until the store opens."

"Yes, but it has to be something that won't interfere with getting this place ready. Not to mention, with Christmas over, things here in Oaks Crossing will be slowing way down. Local businesses aren't exactly hiring right now."

"I don't know about that," he commented, letting out a grin. "You still remember how to wait tables?"

She stared at him as if he'd sprouted another head. "What?"

"One of our servers is a college girl headed back to school at the end of January, so I could use some breakfast help at the Oaks. Y'know, a country girl who doesn't mind getting up early and charming our customers into buying an extra order of bacon."

"You'd hire me?"

Her astonishment caught him off guard, and he frowned. "Any reason I shouldn't?"

"Well, not really. Except that we don't like each other."

"I kinda thought we'd put all that kid nonsense behind us. I mean, I did offer to escort you to a women's prison," he said with a wry grin.

"Yeah, you did," she commented in a disbelieving voice. "I still don't understand why."

"Let's call it a peace offering. In the spirit of the season." When she didn't respond, he decided to press a little. "We're not ten anymore, Erin. Or sixteen. I like my independence, too, and it kills me to rely on anyone for anything. But right now, to get what we want, we're gonna have to swallow our pride and help each other."

"I guess you've got a point. Parker leaves for school around eight, so I could come in right after that. At least it's a short commute," she added in the sassy tone he was starting to like just a little too much.

Getting to his feet, he said, "That's the spirit. If we can stick it out through the winter, in the end I think we'll both be happy with the end result."

"Me here with my new business and Parker, and you back in Minnesota. Right?"

He wasn't sure why she'd phrased it that

way, but he couldn't argue with the accuracy of her statement, so he nodded. "Right."

Looking down at the beat-up door he was using as a tabletop, she scratched at a fleck of old paint on the surface. When she lifted her head, there was a disconcerting spark in her eyes. "Do you think you'd ever consider moving back here?"

"Not a chance," he answered reflexively, the same way he'd done since graduating from high school. "I have a great job up north, and once I get my building designer's certification, I'll have the kind of career I've always wanted. Natalie's got her family now, so once Mom's feeling better, I'm outta here."

The spark dimmed considerably, and she turned her attention back to the shop design. "It seems to me that if we adjust the width of these display shelves, people would have more space to walk in between them."

And, just like that, she was back to business. Cam couldn't figure out what that very personal detour had been about, but apparently she was satisfied with his answer. The trouble was, even though leaving Oaks Crossing had been his plan all along, now he was starting to wonder.

Was it really the best way forward, or should he reconsider?

Recognizing that now was not the right time for soul-searching, he followed Erin's lead and got to work building a materials list. When Parker bounded downstairs to lend a hand, the three of them strolled around the store, chalking various areas on the floor and debating how much space each section would need. To Cam's surprise, the kid was actually helpful, especially when it came to designing the petting corral.

"The fence should be this high," he suggested, holding a hand at his shoulder height. "And have one of those locking pool gates so little kids can't open it by mistake and let all the animals out."

"That's good," Erin approved, making a note on her clipboard. "It should also be low enough that if there's a problem, parents can lift their kids out quickly."

"You mean a problem like not wanting to let go of a cute beagle?" Cam teased with a chuckle.

"I can only hope we have to deal with lots of those. Not just so the store is a success, but so all those poor darlings find good homes."

"Everyone needs someone to love them," Parker agreed in a voice that sounded way too somber for an eight-year-old.

Smiling, Erin put an arm around his shoulders and gave a light squeeze. "We'll do our best."

Cam got the distinct impression that she was referring to more than pet adoptions, and he felt an unfamiliar twang in his chest. Parker didn't know it, but he'd become the prize in an emotional tug-of-war between the woman who'd dumped him into the foster system and the one fiercely determined to rescue him from it.

If Erin couldn't convince Parker's mom to relinquish custody of him, Cam hated to consider what might happen to the bright, sensitive boy he'd become so fond of.

"All right," he said briskly to drag himself out of his brooding, "this looks like a good start. I've got stuff to do over in Rockville, so I'll stop by the home improvement store and pick up these supplies for you. When I was working on the diner, I opened a contractor's account there, so if I buy them, you'll get a discount."

"That's great, Cam. Thank you." Erin added a grateful smile and handed over her list. "In the meantime, we'll get this place all cleaned up so it's ready for construction this afternoon."

She patted his shoulder with a look of encouragement that made it plain she'd guessed what his errand was all about, and that he didn't want to discuss it. How she knew that was beyond him, but he appreciated the supportive gesture all the same.

During the drive, he ran several scenarios through his head but finally stopped because every one of them ended badly. He strolled into the Farmer's Grill fifteen minutes early, figuring he'd park himself at a table and gain the upper hand in this very awkward situation with his father. Best laid plans, he thought when he noticed the tall businessman in a booth near the door talking on a sleek black cell phone.

When he saw Cam, he ended the call and stood to greet him. "Thanks for coming."

He started to offer his hand, then seemed to think better of it and instead motioned Cam to the other bench. The waitress took their drink orders and once she left, the man he'd spent most of his life hating folded his hands on the table and fixed him with a woeful expression.

"There's no way for me to apologize enough for what I did to you, Natalie and your mother."

Cam refused to take that bait, so he just sat back and crossed his arms in what he hoped came across as a casual but doubtful pose.

After they'd ordered lunch, his host tried again. "But I'd like to try."

"Okay."

Cam was waiting for him to suggest a check or some other form of payment that would get him off the hook. What he did instead was the last thing Cam could have anticipated, despite all his pondering on the way here. "All those years ago, I was a very unhappy young man who wasn't ready to take responsibility for myself, much less anyone else. After I left here, I spent a lot of time drifting from place to place, searching for what was missing from my life."

The confession struck uncomfortably close to things Cam had felt from time to time but had never given words to. The idea that he'd somehow inherited his father's selfish streak didn't sit well with him, and he struggled to keep his voice civil. "If you're looking for sympathy from me, you're wasting your time. You had everything most people would give anything to have, and you walked away from it."

"I know, and I regret that every day. I used to think that in time I'd move past the guilt, but as I get older it only gets worse. This time of year is the worst, because most folks are with their families and I'm alone."

Now it made sense, Cam thought bitterly. He'd come back because he'd met someone and wanted to marry her, start a new family that suited him better than the old one. "So you're here for a divorce?"

"Absolutely not," his father spat out, anger flaring in the dark eyes that were so much like the ones Cam saw in the mirror every morning. "Why would you even suggest that?"

"I don't know, *Dad*," Cam shot back, adding plenty of venom to the name. "You tell me."

The waitress returned with their lunches, which gave him a chance to get a better hold on his temper. Erin wasn't the only one with a quick trigger. Why she'd popped into his mind at that moment was a mystery to him, but the brief detour had the welcome effect of cooling him down enough to keep from throttling the man seated across the table.

"I came," his father continued, "to make amends."

The simple, heartfelt answer had a ring of truth in it, but Cam was still skeptical. "Why now?"

"The pastor at the church I've been going to has been counseling me about my…" he paused for a grimace "…shameful past. I can't change what I did back then, but I've missed you all very much, and I'm praying that we can somehow find a way to be a family again."

Cam knew his mother had sent up the same prayer every day for nearly eighteen years. Because, for some reason he'd never understood, she still loved David Stewart and had never lost faith in the idea that he could be the husband and father they all needed. For his own part, Cam still wasn't sure about it, but he had to give the guy credit. He was standing firm and taking every hit Cam threw at him, refusing to back down from a fight.

Confronted by his special brand of unyielding opposition, most people he knew would have given up and turned tail a long time ago.

And then, for some reason, his earlier comment to Erin floated into his mind and he extended his hand across the table. "In the spirit of the season, I'll give it a try."

As they shook, gratitude flooded his father's eyes, and he gave Cam a tentative smile. "I won't let you down this time. I promise."

Cam had his doubts, but he'd already given his word, so he kept them to himself. But if things ended up the way he thought they would, David Stewart would have to run a lot farther away than Michigan.

Chapter Six

That evening, it was almost nine when Cam finished the year-end inventory at the restaurant and headed for home. It had been a long, productive day, but he was bushed and long past ready for some peace and quiet. He'd expected to find the house dark and silent, but instead the Christmas lights were on and strains of "Auld Lang Syne" drifted through the open front door. As he came up the front walk, he stopped abruptly, hardly able to believe his eyes.

There, on the front porch, sat his parents. His father was singing quietly in a passable baritone while his mother looked on from her wheelchair with a contented smile. The sight of them together again after all these years did something funky to Cam's heart, and he took a deep breath to regain his composure.

When he'd been younger, he'd often imagined them reuniting and making their family whole. But that dream had died long ago, and he'd learned to function without the solid foundation buddies like Drew had taken for granted. Somewhere deep inside him, Cam felt that hopeful child coming to life, eager to embrace what he'd given up wishing for.

Putting the foolish notion aside, he climbed the front steps and greeted Mom with a kiss on the cheek before taking a seat on the old swing. "How're you feeling tonight?"

"Just fine," she replied, adding a lopsided smile. "Did you have a good turnout at the diner today?"

"Yeah. Everyone who came in said to give you their best wishes for a Happy New Year."

She sighed. "I miss seeing them."

"I know, but the doctor said you needed to keep things calm a while longer," he reminded her as gently as he could. Having run a busy restaurant for so many years, he understood that it was tough for her to be isolated from the Oaks Crossing social scene she enjoyed so much.

"Maybe it's time for less of that," Dad suggested, "and more visitors."

Coming from anyone else, the comment wouldn't have bothered him in the least. He might even have agreed. But because the source was his long-absent father, it sounded like criticism of how Cam and Natalie had handled Mom's recovery.

Tamping down a flare of temper, he did his best to appear reasonable. "Since I haven't got a degree in medicine, I figure it's best to follow the orders of someone who does."

"Of course," his father backpedaled. "I didn't mean to step on any toes."

"It's easy for you to second-guess. You weren't there in the hospital when she couldn't recognize her own children or sit up long enough to sip water from a cup."

"Cameron." Although her voice was still far from its usual strength, her disapproving frown had nothing to do with the stroke she'd suffered. "What's done is done."

"So you forgive him, just like that?" She nodded, and despite his vow to be patient, he lost it. Standing to his full height, he glared down at the man who'd left a twelve-year-old boy to be in charge of the family he'd decided had no place in his life anymore. "Well, I'm sorry, but I can't do it. This is Mom's house, and if she wants to have you as a guest, I can't stop her. But I've got no intention of staying to watch."

Without waiting for the reprimand he probably deserved, he stalked back to his truck and kicked up plenty of gravel peeling out of the driveway. He had no clue where he was going, but he felt a bone-deep need to be somewhere—anywhere—else. As he drove away, it struck him that with the Christmas lights and porch decorations, the old homestead looked as bright and inviting as any home in town.

Sadly, the reality was anything but cheerful. Against all logic, his mother seemed determined to embrace the man who'd abandoned her, allowing him back into her trust without hesitation. And suddenly, he understood why.

She still loved David Stewart.

In spite of everything he'd done—and hadn't done—her feelings for him hadn't changed. How was that even possible? he wondered. Of anyone, she'd lost the most when he left, humiliating her in front of her friends and family in a way that no woman should ever have to endure.

Still searching for some kind of explanation, he found himself at the blinking traffic light in the village's tiny business district. He didn't remember heading in this direction on purpose, a sure sign that he had no business driving in his current state. He pulled to the curb and shut off the engine, gripping the wheel and taking deep breaths to settle a storm of emotions raging beyond his control.

When he heard a tap on the window, he glanced out to find Erin there with a flashlight, peering in at him in obvious concern. He cranked the old window down and gave her what he hoped was something like a grin. "Hey."

"Hey yourself. Are you having car trouble?"

"Parent trouble," he corrected her wryly. "Sorry if I woke you."

"I was up reading the new book Lily got me for Christmas. Parker passed out on the way home from the mall, so I've been enjoying the peace and quiet."

The reference to calm surroundings jerked Cam back to the argument with his father, and with great effort he shook off the lingering anger that was hanging on him like a tenacious linebacker. "Sounds nice."

She studied him for a long moment, then said, "I've got shortbread cookies and cocoa. You want some?"

Her casual offer defused some of this temper, and he chuckled. "Do I look like I need it?"

"Well, yeah. That and a patient ear."

"Since when do you have one of those?"

"It comes with the mom package."

Since he didn't have any better ideas, he closed the window and dragged himself from the cab to follow her upstairs. "I won't stay long. I'd hate to get the hens clucking about how late I showed up here."

"You know," she said with a cheeky grin, "there's something wrong with the water pipes in the kitchen. They've been dripping all night, and I'm afraid they'll ruin the floor if they're not fixed right away."

"So you're gonna tell folks I'm a hero?"

"Don't get carried away, hotshot," she warned as she reached into a cupboard and took out a mug shaped like Santa's bag of toys. "There's a real leak, but I put a bucket under it. I was going to call you in the morning."

"I should've known you wouldn't lie to anyone," he said, ducking under the sink to see what was going on.

"I'm guessing you have."

"Sure. Sometimes it's easier."

She didn't respond to that, and he looked up to find her studying him again. "What?"

"Did you ever think that if you didn't take the easy route, things would go better for you in the long run?"

"Nope." Standing, he wiped his damp palms on a towel. "This connection just needs to be tightened and it'll be good as new. I've got a wrench in my office, so I'll get it and be right back."

"Okay. Thanks."

She was giving him a strange look, and even though he knew he should leave it alone, he felt compelled to say, "I'm not a bad guy, Erin. I just don't like a lot of complications in my life. You can understand that, right?"

"I suppose, but you've always done things your own way no matter what anyone said. Why do you care what I think?"

Good question. While he didn't go out of his way to frustrate people, he didn't kowtow to them, either. If they liked him, fine. If they didn't, that was their choice. Because of his rocky personal history, he'd learned not to worry all that much about how other folks viewed him. *After all*, he mused darkly, *you didn't get to be the black sheep of your family by accident.*

"I don't," he finally said. "I just wanna make sure it's accurate."

"Because?"

She was driving at something, but for the life of him he couldn't figure out what. They stood toe to toe, her looking up at him without a hint of the uncertainty he normally saw when people were this close to him. Big as he was, he knew he intimidated people, and he frequently used that to his advantage.

But not Erin. Clearly unfazed, she held his gaze, waiting for him to answer her. He searched for something reasonable to say and finally came up with an explanation he thought she'd accept. "Because we're friends, and I do care what my friends think of me."

She chewed on that for a few seconds before nodding. "Okay. That I believe."

"Good, 'cause it's the truth."

He strolled toward a door in the far wall of the kitchen and took out his keys. When he unlocked the door, she gasped. "That leads to the second floor of the Oaks?"

"This is the common wall between the two buildings. Where did you think it went?"

"I haven't had time to breathe, much less wonder about random doors in the building. Can you unlock it from either side?"

For a moment, he couldn't imagine why she'd ask him that. Then it occurred to him that she was a single woman with a young child. Even though they lived in the safest place he'd ever been to, he understood her concern. "After I get back, we'll lock the door and I'll give you both keys so no one can get in here from the other side. Will that make you more comfortable?"

"Much. Thank you."

"You're welcome. I'm just sorry I didn't think of it before."

Cam stepped through the door and picked up his toolbox, locking the door as he came back. As he'd promised, he handed Erin both keys before sliding under the sink to tighten the leaky joint. When the drip stopped, he wiped down the pipes and waited a minute or so to make sure he'd solved the problem.

"All set," he announced as he got to his feet and closed the cabinet doors. "Anything else?"

"That's it for now." Handing him the outlandish mug, she sat on one of the stools at the counter.

He took the one next to her and plucked a cookie from a plate decorated with candy canes and silver stars. "This is smaller, but it reminds me of the kitchen at the farm."

"Parker said the same thing yesterday," she told him with a smile. "He said it makes this place feel more like Grammy's, and it's his favorite spot in the apartment."

Cam chuckled around a mouthful of crumbs. "That kid is something else. Have you told him about meeting with his mother?"

"I don't know how. I'm afraid if I mention

it to him beforehand, he won't take it well. Once I know for sure what she wants, I guess I'll have to sit down and lay it all out for him. I'm not looking forward to it."

"Has he ever told anyone what really happened to him?"

"Not to my knowledge. I figure that when he's ready, he'll tell me about it. Until then, I'm just doing everything I can to make sure he knows that I love him and I'm never going to give up on him."

Big boys need that, too.

The thought came out of nowhere, and Cam lifted his mug for a long swallow of cocoa to keep this very observant woman from seeing his emotions in his eyes. He wasn't sure what was going on with him, but he couldn't deny that sometime between the old year and the new, things between Erin and him had changed.

Some guys would've taken that and run with it. But not him. And especially not with her.

It was nearly an hour's drive to the facility where Lynn Smith was being held. Medium security, Alice had assured Erin, which meant that the people there weren't exactly guiltless, but they hadn't murdered anyone, either. Unfortunately, that was a small comfort to a girl who'd been so by-the-book, she'd never even skipped class in high school.

"It's gonna be fine," Cam declared as he drove past the guard station and parked in the visitors' lot. "She'll be on one side of the table, we'll be on the other. She just wants to meet you and see for herself what kind of person you are."

"Why?" Erin asked for the countless time.

Slanting her a look, he gave her one of those almost grins he wore so often. "Are you seriously asking me to explain why a woman is doing something? I'm divorced for a reason."

"Silly me." She tried to laugh, but it came out sounding more like a shaky cough. Staring at the imposing brick building, she took a deep breath that didn't help settle her nerves even the tiniest bit. "I'm really scared about doing this. What if I say the wrong thing and she hates me?"

Cam angled in his seat to face her squarely. "You're not on trial here, Erin. If anything, she should be worried about meeting you."

"You think so?"

"Sure. You've got a great family, a nice place to live and your own business. Not to mention a little boy who thinks you hung the moon. Most folks would think you've got it all, and they'd be pretty jealous of your success."

Erin hadn't thought of herself that way, and hearing her accomplishments laid out was a real eye-opener for her. Fingering her father's oversize watch, she said, "I'm just trying to do what my parents taught me."

"Maybe that woman in there didn't have anyone to teach her the right way to live, so she screwed up her life. Your job—" he pointed at her for emphasis "—is to make sure Parker doesn't suffer for her mistakes any more than he already has."

Cam had a real knack for cutting through all the nonsense and getting to the heart of a problem. His direct manner could be tough to swallow, but as off balance as she was feeling right now, Erin appreciated him being so firm with her. "You're right. Let's go get this over with."

Inside the entryway, they went through security measures that reminded her of an airport, and a guard recited a list of things they shouldn't do while visiting. From memory. It struck Erin that while this was her first trip to a place like this, for some people it was a way of life. The thought of doing this every day was sobering, to say the least.

Finally they were cleared and given badges that identified them as visitors. A middle-aged guard led them down a hallway toward a set of double doors that had large windows in them.

When they arrived, she turned to Erin with a motherly look. "You haven't said a single word, hon. Is this your first time here?"

"Yes, it is."

"Nervous?" Erin nodded, and the woman smiled. "I've worked here almost twenty years, and we've never had a problem between an inmate and any of our guests. Does that help?"

Erin picked up on the carefully worded phrasing and realized the guard was going out of her way to be truthful. So, strange as it seemed, the precise statement boosted her confidence a smidge. "A little. Thank you."

Satisfied, their escort eyed Cam warily. "I don't imagine I could convince you to stay out here while the two ladies talk."

"No, ma'am."

"All right," she conceded with a sigh. "Just be prepared for some gawking. We don't get many as handsome as you in here."

"Hear that?" he whispered to Erin as they entered the visiting area. "She thinks I'm handsome."

The delighted gleam in his eye was kind of cute, and despite the fact that she was still very much on edge, Erin managed to smile at him as they sat down. "I'm sure most women do."

"Not you, though," he went on in the same teasing voice. "Why is that?"

"I know you too well."

That only made him chuckle, and she rolled her eyes at the ceiling. The man was hopeless, but there was no denying that he had his charms. After all, he'd given up most of his day to keep her company during her grim errand. In her mind, that earned him all kinds of points.

A slight blonde woman dressed in an orange jumpsuit approached the table, and Cam stood halfway up before a guard glared him back into his seat.

"Sorry," he said, holding up a hand. "Just a habit."

"Someone raised you right," Lynn Smith said, giving him an approving once-over before taking the lone chair on the other side of the table.

They weren't allowed to shake hands, so Erin rushed straight into the introductions, hoping she didn't sound as nervous as she was feeling. When she was finished, she searched her frazzled brain for something else to say. She drew a total blank and flashed Cam a *help me* look.

Leaning back in his chair, he crossed a boot over his knee like the three of them were shooting the breeze over lunch at the Oaks Café. "So, Lynn, where are you from?"

"Kansas originally. How about you?"

"Kentucky, born and raised. Erin's family owns and runs a horse farm near Louisville, and mine are restaurant people."

She gave Erin an assessing look. "You live on a farm?"

Finally, her manners kicked in, and she replied, "Actually, I moved into town recently to open a pet store. A few years ago I started a nonprofit animal shelter that rescues unwanted pets and rehabilitates other animals before releasing them back into the wild."

"Interesting." Lynn's tone made it clear that she was making a concerted effort to be polite, and she quickly got to the heart of why Erin was there. "Did you bring a picture of my son with you?"

In answer, Erin slid the approved photo across the table and folded her hands tightly on the scarred wooden surface. Awkward didn't begin to describe this situation, and she kept having to remind herself to breathe. Lynn studied the picture for several seconds, her neutral expression revealing nothing about what she might be feeling.

She pushed the image back toward Erin with a faint smile. "He looks good."

"He is good," Erin assured her. "And he's doing well in school, too."

"What did he get for Christmas?"

What an odd question, Erin thought. What difference did that make? Being a good student was far more significant than how many video games he owned. Then again, she was here to mollify a stranger with a troubled past, not make things more difficult than they already were. "My younger brother bought him a remote control helicopter that Parker really likes, and—"

"What did *you* get him?" Lynn interrupted impatiently. "Did you buy him clothes and books, or did you get him something he actually wanted?"

"He loves science, so I gave him a chemistry set and a small telescope so we can look at the stars. Now that it gets dark earlier in the evening, we're tracking the moon's phases every night and plotting its position at an astronomy website we found online."

Lynn blinked, then shook her head with a rueful grin. "I've got no idea what you just said, but it sounds pretty smart to me. Does he have his own room at your place?"

"Yes."

"What's it like?"

Erin described it to her, and again Lynn seemed to approve, if a bit reluctantly. Then her eyes lit on something, and for the first time her harsh features softened. "Is that a cross you're wearing?"

"Yes." Erin lifted it clear of her collar so Lynn could see it better. "My parents gave it to me when I was baptized, and I've worn it ever since."

"You've got a good family. Better than the one I had, that's for sure." She angled a glance at Cam. "What about you?"

Erin expected him to balk at the question, insist that it didn't matter because the two of them weren't a couple and his religious views weren't any of her business. To her astonishment, he quietly said, "There's better families than us, and there's worse."

"An honest man," Lynn commented wryly. "And here I thought they all died out a long time ago."

"There's still a few of us dinosaurs around."

"Not in my world." A guard sidled over to give them the five-minute warning, and Lynn suddenly got very serious. Still focused on Cam, she demanded, "What's your involvement with Parker?"

"He's a great kid, and I enjoy spending time with him."

"So you two aren't dating or anything?"

"We grew up together," he replied evenly. "We're just friends."

His answer seemed to satisfy her, and Erin wondered when they were going to get to the part where Lynn agreed to let her adopt Parker. Instead, she said, "A lifetime of bad decisions landed me in this awful place, but I found something here I'd never had before. Our chaplain is a good, caring man who's been showing me a better way to live."

She paused, and Erin realized that she was waiting for a response. "That's good."

Resting her hand on the table, she showed Erin the small tattoo of a cross on her left ring finger. "I'm not allowed any pretty jewelry, so I did this to show God I understand what He wants from me, and that I'm willing to do it."

The hopeful confession should have been inspiring, but it could have horrible consequences for Parker, and Erin's heart sank to the floor. For all the mistakes she'd confessed to making, Lynn was clearly on the road to redeeming herself, at least in her own eyes. Struggling to put her own misgivings aside, Erin managed to say, "I'm glad to hear that."

The guard strolled over again, and Lynn

sighed before standing up. "That's my cue. Thanks for coming to see me."

"What about Parker?" Erin blurted in desperation.

"I'll have to pray about that. You understand, don't you?"

She most certainly did not, but Erin knew only too well she'd get nowhere trying to bully someone whose violent past had landed her in prison. Summoning the professional but friendly expression she'd perfected for use on demanding attorneys, she nodded. "Of course."

"I'll be in touch."

With that frustratingly vague promise, Lynn gave Erin a wan smile and followed the guard through a door on the far wall. While it was open, Erin glimpsed a long, antiseptic-looking hallway with two long rows of metal doors and nothing else. Despite the roller-coaster ordeal she'd just been through, knowing that Lynn would be spending years more in that stark environment made her sad.

But not half as sad as being escorted from the facility with no concrete answer about Parker's future, she amended bitterly. What on earth was she supposed to do now?

Back in Cam's truck, she stared out the window to make it plain to him that she didn't want to talk. In usual Cam fashion, he honored her unspoken wishes, but after half an hour, he said, "I'm starving. How 'bout you?"

"Not really." Checking her watch, she added, "Parker will be home from school soon. It's his first day back after vacation, so I want to be there."

"For him or for you?"

"What's that supposed to mean?"

"He didn't know where you were going today, or why," Cam reminded her gently, acting as if she hadn't just bitten his head off. "He doesn't strike me as the kind of kid who needs babying, but if you want to see him to make yourself feel better, I get it."

Delivered with a strong dose of sympathy, the logical explanation soothed her nerves a bit, and she admitted, "You're right, it's for me. And I'm sorry I barked at you. It's been a long, stressful day."

"After not much sleep last night, I'd imagine." Angling a grin her way, he winked. "Don't worry, bug. I can take it."

"I really wish you'd quit calling me that."

"I know."

He gave her an unapologetic grin that made her laugh in spite of herself. "You're hopeless."

"I've been called worse."

"I don't doubt it."

"Y'know," he began, resting his arm across the back of the old bench seat, "I've been mulling over how this all went down, and I've got a theory. Wanna hear it?"

Figuring he knew a lot more about the seedier side of people than she did, she swiveled to face him. "Sure."

"I think Lynn is coming up on some kind of review that will either set an early release date or force her to serve her full sentence."

"So you don't believe she's going to pray about it?"

"Not hardly," he scoffed. "I believe she's gonna pray that she gets released early, but the legal system might have more to do with that than she wants to admit. At least to you."

"That's a pretty cynical attitude."

"I've worked with ex-cons who had a real gift for lying to themselves and everyone around them. How 'bout you?"

Erin had never met anyone who'd been in such serious trouble with the law, and she acknowledged that she'd have to take his word on this one. "So, if she's getting out soon, she'll want Parker back?"

"And if she's gonna be in there for a few more years, she might decide that by the time she gets out, he'll be a teenager who hates her for abandoning him."

Erin acknowledged that Cam knew what he was talking about, from the kid's perspective. "Do you think things would've been different if your dad had come back earlier?"

He didn't look over at her, but she noticed the firming of his jaw and how his hands gripped the wheel a little more tightly. Reining in his infamous temper instead of letting it fly, she mused. Interesting.

"I'm not sure," he confided in a thoughtful tone. "A few days ago, I would've said no. Seeing Mom and him together the other night made me furious, but once I calmed down, I realized I can't keep her from loving him. But that doesn't mean I have to forgive him for what he did to us."

"I'm confused. You told him he could come by."

"I didn't think he'd drive right over to visit her when I was gone."

"With all the health problems she's had recently, I could understand him being anxious to see for himself that she was doing better," Erin pointed out. "Maybe he wanted to see you, too, but you weren't there."

"Don't be getting all logical on me," he growled. "I know it's stupid, but that's how I feel."

"What about Natalie?"

He shrugged. "She thinks Mom should do whatever she wants. Nat doesn't remember him all that well, so it's not like she missed him or anything."

"But you did." Erin filled in the very large blank he'd left hanging in the middle of their conversation. She had wonderful memories of her dad, and she couldn't imagine what it must have been like for Cam to know he had a father who'd chosen not to be part of his life. "Maybe part of you still does."

"Whatever."

The simple, careless response did nothing to mask how he actually felt. He'd done so much for Parker and her, she wished there was a way she could help him come to terms with the unwieldy position his family was in. Since there wasn't, she opted to end the discussion by turning on the radio.

As they turned off the highway and headed for Oaks Crossing, he surprised her once again. "I'll try."

"Try what?" she prodded.

He groaned. "Are you really gonna make me say it?"

"You're a man of your word. If you say it, I know you'll do it. If it helps any, I honestly believe putting away the past is what's best for all of you," she added in a gentler voice.

"You're a real pain, you know that?"

"Isn't that why you started calling me 'bug' in the first place?"

"Yeah, but you do have a point. This time," he added with a scowl. When she didn't reply, he heaved a long-suffering male sigh. "Fine. I'll try to be more open-minded about my dad. Happy?"

"Yes. And I know your mom will really appreciate you doing this for her."

His dark look mellowed into the kind of smile that reminded her that under all that bluster was a great big heart of gold. "If you keep telling me that, I just might be able to stand having him around again."

"Deal."

On a chilly afternoon in late January, Cam was double-checking the most recent shipment the contractors' supply store had dropped off at the storefront that a huge sign hanging on the door proudly identified as The Future Home of Pampered Paws. Strolling around the impressive stacks of lumber and Sheetrock, he counted items and checked them off before moving on to the boxes of nails and other hardware. To his amazement, everything down to the last screw was accounted for. He wasn't a superstitious guy by nature, but he couldn't help thinking this was a promising way to start the new year.

The ceiling blowout had taken more work than he'd anticipated, but now the space was flooded with light from the reclaimed windows, soaring up into the hand-hewn oak rafters with the rustic look he'd envisioned weeks ago. By some remarkable twist of fortune, he and Erin were equally pleased with the result, and he'd quickly gotten her to sign off on that portion of his task list before she changed her mind.

When the school bus pulled up outside, he glanced out the front window to see a dozen kids pile out and wave to each other before scattering to the right and left to walk home. The sight of them sparked an idea, and he jotted a note on his clipboard: *half-price ice cream/snacks for school kids*. It might not amount to much on a daily basis, but over the course of a month, he wouldn't be surprised to find that the extra business would fill the dead spot the Oaks Café normally experienced between lunch and dinner.

Parker swung the door open, his face lighting up when he saw Cam. "Whoa, that's a lotta stuff."

"We're gonna need it," Cam told him, glancing back at Erin when she appeared in the newly framed doorway that led into what would soon be her office. "Boss Lady has big plans for this place."

"Boss Lady," she echoed with a smirk. "I like it."

"I thought you might."

"How was your day?" she asked as she slid off Parker's backpack and zipped it open to rummage through the sheaf of loose papers he'd brought home from school.

"Awesome," he replied with a bright grin. "We got the science fair forms today. Can we fill them out now?"

"Absolutely. Do you want to help?" she asked Cam. He recognized a pity invitation when he heard one, but it still felt nice to be included.

"Sure." Clearing a spot on the workbench, he pulled up a three-legged stool and sat down. "Let's see what you've got."

"Mr. Simms gave us a list of things to choose from," Parker explained as he handed a collection of stapled papers to Erin. "But I came up with my own idea, and he really liked it."

"Does it involve going to the moon?" she teased with a smile.

"Maybe someday," he replied eagerly. "I wanna build an engine that runs on something besides gas. We saw a video about them in school, and how good they are for the envinement."

"Environment," she corrected him patiently, waiting while he repeated the ten-dollar word back to her. "That's it. What kind of fuel did you have in mind?"

His freckled face crinkled while he considered his answer. "The video showed some made from corn, but it's past harvest season, so there won't be any more of that at the farm." Looking over at Cam, he asked, "Do you know something else we could use?"

And just like that, Cam realized he'd been promoted from interested observer to outright participant. Because he'd never been involved with a child older than his adorable, babbly niece Sophie, complicated school projects weren't exactly his specialty. But seeing Parker looking at him with hope shining in his blue eyes, he saw something he hadn't expected to find in this bright, engaging boy.

He saw himself.

Eager and full of enthusiasm, despite all the hardships he'd endured. Somehow Parker had come through all that, emerging out the other side with an upbeat view of life plenty of adults—including Cam—would do well to imitate. And so, because he simply couldn't imagine disappointing his excited apprentice, Cam delved into his own experience for an option.

Inspiration struck, and he grinned. "What about biodiesel?"

"What's that?" Parker asked.

"I don't know all that much about it, but a buddy of mine up in Minnesota converted a lawn tractor to use diesel fuel he made in his shop. We'd have to research the details, but I know he started with used cooking oil from restaurants around town. He got it for free, because they usually paid to have it collected by a recycler and were happy to get rid of the stuff."

He left off there, and Erin picked up his train of thought without missing a beat. "And we know someone who has a lot of used cooking oil just hanging around in his fryers. That's perfect, Cam. Great idea."

To his surprise, her approval felt just as good to him as Parker's. Their relationship was challenging, at best, so the gradual shift in her attitude toward him over the past couple of weeks had confused him at first. But as they talked through strategies for how to make Parker's project a winner, they settled into a comfortable rhythm of give and take. It wasn't as hard as he would've thought, seeing as they were both focused on encouraging Parker and what would certainly be considered a revolutionary science project for a third grader.

"I think there's an ancient lawn mower in the shed at my mom's house," Cam told him, thinking out loud. "I'm not sure if it still runs, but those two-cycle motors aren't too complicated. With a little oil and elbow grease, we can probably get it working."

"A small engine would be good," Parker agreed eagerly, sketching it onto the drawing. "Whatever we make has to fit on two school desks so there's room for all the projects in the room where they do the judging."

"You'd want to include the filtering system to show how it works," Cam added, tapping the paper. "Otherwise, all folks will see is a motor spinning away till it runs out of gas."

"Biodiesel," Parker corrected him, adding a nondescript block to represent the filter none of them had the first clue about how to build.

Even though he'd just been schooled by an eight-year-old, Cam couldn't keep back a grin. "Right. So, what are you gonna call this display?"

"I don't know yet. I'll come up with something."

Cam didn't doubt that for a second. And as he watched Erin and Parker pencil details on the plan, an odd thought crept into his mind for the first time.

A stranger walking past the shop would assume the three of them were a family. A mom, dad and son sitting in the unfinished space with their heads together over a pile of homework. Even odder, after a month of hanging out with them on a more or less daily basis, he was beginning to feel that way himself.

Maybe it was his father's continued visits to Oaks Crossing or the mushy traditions that came along with the holiday season. Whatever the explanation was, he couldn't deny that he'd begun to think of these two as more than just another set of tenants.

And somehow, when he wasn't paying attention, Erin had become more to him than a friend. How else would he explain accompanying her to see Lynn Smith, or why he'd opened up to her about painful things he'd never even considered discussing with anyone else? Somewhere deep inside, he'd decided that he could trust her to listen without judging him and try to understand where he was coming from, even if she saw the situation differently. Even more incredible, he was confident that he could lean on her and she wouldn't buckle under the pressure.

He was accustomed to being the one people

turned to for support, tackling problems on his own because that approach to life had always worked best for him. The fact that he and Erin were there for each other was both astonishing and terrifying.

Because when you gave up your independence and started relying on someone, you gave them the power to destroy you when they left. Since they'd both made it clear that they weren't interested in any kind of entanglements right now, getting in any deeper with Erin and her endearing foster son was out of the question.

For as long as he could remember, Cam had done everything in his power to prove that when it came to relationships, he wasn't his father's son. His divorce had made him gunshy about making such a serious commitment again, especially if it involved a child. While part of him believed he'd enjoy being part of the cozy family circle Erin was building, the more pragmatic side of him knew that allowing himself to become part of it could only end badly. For all of them.

With that decision made, he reluctantly left Erin and Parker to their planning and got back to work hanging the door to her new office.

Chapter Seven

As she'd arranged with Cam, on the first Monday in February Erin walked Parker to the bus and then quickly covered the few yards to start her new job. She hadn't waitressed in years, but she ate at the Oaks Café frequently enough that she was not only familiar with the varied menus, she knew everyone who was sitting in the dining room when she arrived. Cam was on the phone but glanced over when she entered, giving her a subtle nod before turning his back to resume his conversation.

Apparently, the brief exchange was all the employee orientation she was going to get, she mused with a grin. It was nice to know her boss had so much faith in her ability to come in and hit the ground running. She looked around to get a feel for what was going on, then grabbed a couple of menus and headed for a table near the window. On her way, she snatched a pot of coffee and approached two of her father's old friends with a bright smile.

"Good morning, you two," she greeted them while she set down their menus and filled their cups. "How have you been?"

"You workin' here now?" Pete Miller asked, cocking his head to the side.

Mindful of the fact that he was nearly deaf in his left ear, she leaned forward a bit so he could hear her more clearly. "Yes, I am, at least until Pampered Paws is up and running."

"How's it going for you over there?" his slightly younger brother, Frank, asked, nodding at the wall that separated her business space from the diner.

"We've got a plan all put together, and with Cam's help we should be ready to open in a month or so. I'm going to run an open house for local folks the weekend before our official opening. I hope you'll come by and see for yourselves what we've been up to."

Having been an office assistant of one kind or another since graduating from high school, Erin was keenly aware that she wasn't a natural-born salesperson like Cam. Because she had no clue about advertising, she was leaving the marketing tasks for the rescue center to Bekah, who excelled at generating ideas and putting them into motion. Promoting her new business felt a little awkward to her right now, but Erin was confident that it would get easier with practice. At least, that's what she kept telling herself.

"Erin!"

At the sound of her name, she turned to find her friend Glenda Rymer hanging out in the entryway. Erin motioned her inside, but Glenda glanced at Cam and shook her head. Intrigued, Erin left the brothers with their menus and went to see what her visitor wanted. When she reached the entrance, she saw what the problem was.

There, sitting politely but alertly beside Glenda, was a German shepherd puppy wearing a navy blue poplin vest that read Service Dog in Training. Cam hadn't said a word, but he was eyeballing the dog with obvious interest.

Careful to approach slowly, Erin kept her voice calm to avoid upsetting the pup. "This must be the famous Bear we've been hearing about. Aren't you a handsome little guy?"

"And at the head of his class," Glenda crowed, as if she was bragging about one of her own kids. "I can't thank you enough for agreeing to puppysit for us, Erin. He's a good boy, but you can't leave a service dog with just anyone."

"It's not a problem at all. Parker was thrilled when Aaron asked him about it, and I think it'll be a great experience for him." Moving slowly, she hunkered down and looked into those bright, intelligent eyes. When he cocked his head at her and offered his paw, she laughed as they shook. "Nice to meet you, Bear."

"He's already had breakfast and a walk, and I emailed you his schedule," Glenda told her as she handed over the leash and a large duffel bag. "He should be fine for an hour or so by himself, but he needs to be around people as much as possible. My sister's wedding is on Saturday, and we'll be home Sunday morning around nine. If you need anything or have any questions, call me anytime. Except during the vows." She giggled. "I'm the matron of honor, so I'll have my hands full of my sister's bouquet. I won't be answering my phone then."

"Got it."

Erin hugged Glenda goodbye and sent another server over to get the Miller brothers' orders. Catching Cam's eye, she pointed next door and got a quick nod. She didn't want Bear feeling hemmed in by closing him in one of the bedrooms, so she shut the interior doors and waited for a few minutes while he sniffed his way through the living area of the apartment. He stopped near a patch of sunlight in front of the bay window and sat, giving her a questioning look.

"Good boy, Bear," she approved with an exaggerated nod to emphasize her words. "That's fine."

His lips crinkled in what she could only term a canine smile. After circling three times, he stretched out on the braided area rug, heaving a contented sigh.

"Best houseguest ever," she murmured on her way down the stairs, making sure the lower door latched firmly behind her. On her phone, she set an alarm that would repeat every hour to remind her to check in with their fuzzy visitor. And then it was back to the salt mines.

When she returned to the diner, Cam met her near the door with a look that was somewhere between stern and amused. It was an odd combination, but somehow on him it worked.

"I'm pretty sure that lease you signed forbids you to have pets," he began in a conversational tone that wouldn't have fooled anyone with half a brain in their head.

"Bear isn't a pet, and he's incredibly well

behaved. I'm just watching him for a friend until Sunday."

She kept her voice low because she didn't want anyone to overhear their conversation and incorrectly assume that Cam was giving her any kind of special treatment. Why that mattered she wasn't entirely certain, but in a town this small the gossip mill churned 24/7. Anyone who valued their reputation kept their personal issues on the hush-hush if it was humanly possible.

"I noticed he's a service dog," Cam went on while he straightened the menus in the rack on the front counter. "Is he being trained for anything in particular?"

"Right now, he's learning how to get along with people and other animals at home and in public. When he's mastered the basics, the trainers will teach him to help with specific tasks."

"That sounds expensive."

"Actually, the group Glenda fosters dogs for is totally volunteer. Back when I was thinking about starting the shelter, I went to a seminar on how to run a successful nonprofit organization." Erin paused, smiling at the memory. "She and I bonded over the worst cup of coffee we'd ever had and snuck out to the gourmet coffee shop next door. We've been friends ever since."

"Your houseguest looks like a purebred to me."

"He is."

"So you're telling me this outfit takes on valuable dogs, trains them as helpers and just hands them to people?" he asked.

"Yes."

That seemed to throw him off balance, and he pulled back in obvious bewilderment. "That's incredible."

"That's what everyone says," she replied with an understanding smile. "But when you see a visually impaired person walking at the mall, or someone in a wheelchair who's able to do things they couldn't manage on their own before, you get why they do it."

Something she'd just said seemed to grab his attention, and his usually reserved manner perked up considerably. Stepping closer, he murmured, "Did you say wheelchair?"

Excitement glittered in those dark eyes, and she immediately understood what he was getting at. "You're thinking your mom might benefit from having a service dog?"

"She hates being cooped up and having to rely on other people to do every last little thing for her." He paused, as if he needed a moment to decide just how much he wanted to share with her.

"Go ahead," she urged gently. "This is me, so whatever it is you don't have to phrase it perfectly. You can just spit it out."

"Well, I hate to admit this," he hedged with a rueful grin, "but Dad had a point about taking her outside for some fresh air during his first visit. I went through the roof when I saw her sitting on the porch on a cool night like that, but it really cheered her up. Even the next day, she seemed more like her old self than she has in a long time."

Erin thought it might have something to do with finally seeing her long-estranged husband again, but out of respect for Cam she kept that opinion to herself. "That makes sense. No one likes to feel helpless, and everyone needs to get outside once in a while."

"Exactly. I keep waiting for her to bounce back from this stroke like she did after her first one, but so far that hasn't happened." Another pause, and this time his look was somber. "I'm starting to worry that if something doesn't change soon, the way she is now might be as far as she's gonna get."

Since she'd never known anyone who'd survived a stroke—much less two in the same year—Erin had no frame of reference for intelligently participating in a discussion like this. She feared that anything she might say about not giving up hope would be received as empty platitudes, so she discarded them and went with honesty. "You've been with her more than anyone, so you could be right."

"If I am, she's gonna need help to make sure she has the best life possible. I have to get back to Minnesota in the spring for the start of building season up north. Even though Natalie and Alex have offered to move in with Mom, they both have full-time jobs and Sophie to take care of besides."

She'd picked up on the fact that he'd pretty much skimmed over his own plans and seemed much more concerned with the arrangements he needed to make for the family he'd be leaving behind. When they'd last discussed him returning to his own life, he'd been adamant about not staying in Oaks Crossing a day longer than was strictly necessary. Coupled with his new—albeit grudging—acceptance of his father's continued presence, the difference from the cool, distant man she'd signed a lease with was remarkable.

Over the past several weeks, Cam had made an incredible amount of personal progress, whether or not he realized it. "If your mother was more independent, it would make things a lot easier for everyone."

"That's what I'm thinking. I'm also thinking that we have to get her name on some kind of list," he added with a frown. "How long do people usually wait for a dog like Bear?"

"I have no idea, but you can ask Glenda when she gets back." Taking out her phone, she scrolled through the address book and found the name she wanted. "I'm sending you her contact info. That way, you can talk to her directly. I'm sure she can answer any questions you, Natalie and Bridget might have about the program. And if there's something she's not familiar with, she'll know someone who's an expert."

"Thanks, Erin. I really appreciate it." Turning to head back toward the kitchen, he glanced back over his shoulder with a grin. "By the way, Bear's welcome to stay with you and Parker anytime. But if he chews it, you fix it."

"Gotcha."

Pointing at him, she gave him a wink that made him laugh. As he walked away, it struck her that the cheerful sound wasn't something she often heard from Cam Stewart. A maddening smirk or a low chuckle, sure, but outright laughter was rarer than the proverbial blue moon.

As she grabbed a coffeepot from the double-decker brewing station and waded back into the breakfast crowd, the wheels in her head started spinning, and she had to force herself to concentrate on her customers.

During a lull before the lunch rush, she sneaked into the store room and dialed Glenda's number.

"Oh, thank you for calling." Her friend sighed. "The kids are all out cold, and Larry hates to talk while he's driving. On top of that, I finished my book ten miles ago and we're still two hours from my sister's house."

The woman sounded absolutely miserable, and Erin asked, "How did it end?"

"The psychotic babysitter did it. But that's not why you're calling. What's up?"

Erin outlined her plan and waited for Glenda to consider it. "That should be fine. I trust your judgment, so as long as you're with Bear and make sure he stays calm, I'm okay with it."

"Awesome. Thank you."

"You've been hanging out with eight year olds for too long," Glenda commented with a laugh. "You're starting to sound just like them. You really need to get out with a grown-up for dinner or something."

What a strange thing for her to say. "I'm at the farm all the time."

"I don't mean your family," Glenda said in a nudging tone. "I was thinking about your hunky landlord. I've heard a lot about him but I'd never met him until today. Yum."

"Cam's just a friend." Glenda let out a derisive snort, and Erin laughed. "No, really. There's nothing romantic going on between us."

"Then you need to get your head examined, sweetie. See you Sunday."

She hung up without saying anything more, and Erin switched her phone off with a frown. First Lynn Smith and now Glenda. For the life of her, she couldn't figure out why folks kept assuming that she and Cam were an item.

Shrugging the question away, she decided there was nothing she could do about other people's impressions. The alarm on her watch sounded, and first she went into the dining room to make sure they hadn't been overrun by customers before heading up to check on her canine guest. He was sprawled out in the sunshine and sound asleep, so she tiptoed out and went back to work.

Cam was pretty sure he could sleep for a month and still not feel rested.

Being in the construction business, he was used to having long, tiring days every week.

On the nights when he had class, they were even longer. But back in Minnesota, he only had himself to worry about, and if the laundry went a few extra days or he ate takeout every night, it didn't matter all that much.

Here in Oaks Crossing, he had plenty of other people to consider, both family and friends. While he was enjoying the uptick in his social life, he wasn't too proud to admit that it was on the verge of wearing him out. But here he was, in the backyard equipment shed, digging up the lawn mower he'd volunteered to let Parker use for his biodiesel project.

When he discovered that the frame had rusted apart, leaving the engine nearly loose on top of the deck, he was a lot happier than he should have been. Normally, it bugged him to no end when things were neglected so long they fell apart. This time it would save him the hassle of dismantling the mower that had been old when he was a kid, so he decided to forget about the reason and appreciate the gift.

A quick yank freed the motor assembly, and he gladly shut and padlocked the door behind him. The shed's interior was a tangled mess of cobwebs, wasps' nests and spare parts, but he didn't have the time or the energy to deal with any of it now. Maybe not ever, he thought as he circled around the house and trudged up the porch steps.

Mom had taken to sitting out there whenever she could, listening to the radio and waving to neighbors as they went by. She'd told him that many detoured to come and chat for a while, and that she felt more involved in the goings-on around town than she had before.

As he joined her, he had to admit she seemed a lot perkier these days. So his father had been right to get her out of the house, after all. Despite the lingering unease they still felt around each other during his visits, Cam was impressed.

"Cam!"

Hearing Parker's shout, he glanced over at the park and saw his carpenter's assistant hustling across Main Street with Erin and Bear trailing close behind him. The young dog didn't run but trotted easily beside Erin, an alert expression on his face. When they reached the Stewarts' yard, she stopped and so did the dog, dropping down to sit beside her without being told.

"I wanted you to meet Bear," Parker said, kneeling to put an arm around his furry buddy. "Isn't he awesome?"

They'd already met, but Cam didn't want to spoil the kid's fun, so he played along. Hunkering down to the shepherd's level, he said, "Nice to see you, Bear."

As he had with Erin, the dog offered a paw, and Cam shook it. The dog's ears twitched when he noticed Mom on the porch, and he looked up at Erin, whining softly.

"I called Glenda earlier, and while we were chatting she told me that he's being trained for a boy in a wheelchair," she explained.

"And you thought Mom should meet him?"

"Yes, but only if you want her to," Erin added hastily.

That she'd go out of her way to help his mother touched him in a way he couldn't begin to describe. Thoughtful and pragmatic, it was a very Erin thing to do, and he appreciated it more than he could possibly say. "I think it's a great idea. Come on up."

Standing, he hung back while the others trooped up the steps. Erin approached his mother easily, as if she was just sitting in a regular chair, and introduced "the guys."

"It's so nice to have company," Mom said quietly, motioning toward the porch swing with a hand that still shook more than he'd like. "Would you like a snack?"

"Thank you, but we're on our way home for dinner," Erin told her. "We were over in the park and thought we'd come by to wish you a belated Happy New Year."

"That's sweet of you," Mom approved, her face crinkling in her usual half smile. Focusing on Parker, she asked, "Did you stay up until midnight?"

He nodded earnestly. "Yes, ma'am, for the first time. It was fun but kinda tiring."

"Most good things are. Like this puppy here," she added with a smile for Bear. "Does he like to chase balls?"

"Yes, ma'am. But he's a very good dog, because he's going to help a little boy in a wheelchair have a better life."

"That's wonderful."

"Bear's great," the boy assured her, eyes shining with enthusiasm. "He and that boy are gonna be real good friends."

While they continued talking, the quilting article his mother had been reading slipped from her lap and landed on the floorboards. Without being prompted, Bear stood and walked across the porch. Picking the magazine up in his teeth, he gently set it on the table and returned to his spot next to Erin. The smooth, careful way he handled the task made it obvious that he'd practiced a similar chore many times and had it down pat.

"Good boy," Erin murmured, scratching between his ears with an approving smile.

When she lifted her head and met Cam's gaze, that smile was still there. Warm and affectionate, it made it easy for him to smile back as he mouthed, "Thank you."

Giving him a wink, she turned her attention back to the discussion that had shifted to Parker's science project.

"How am-ambi…" Mom stammered, hung up in the middle of a word she'd once used so effortlessly. Cam nearly jumped in to finish for her, but Erin stopped him with a subtle shake of her head.

He held his tongue but waited anxiously for his mother to display the frustration that was so common for her these days. Instead, to his astonishment, she firmed her chin in determination and spat out what she'd been trying so hard to say. "Ambitious of you."

"Thank you." Parker beamed proudly. "My teacher said he likes knowing kids want to help keep the planet cleaner."

"Good for you."

"Well," Erin said as she got up, "we really should be going. Dinner's in the Crock-Pot, and Parker has a bunch of homework to do."

Cam silently thanked her for realizing that his mother was starting to fade and stood while they said their goodbyes before walking them down the steps. "Parker, I found that lawn mower engine today. I'll get it cleaned up and bring it by your place in the morning before you go to school."

"Awesome! Thanks, Cam." Wrapping him in a quick hug, the boy grinned up at him like he was Superman. "Can we get started on my project soon?"

"How does tomorrow afternoon sound?"

"Cool. Erin, can I take Bear now?"

"Yes, but calmly."

"Okay."

She handed him the leash, and he headed down the brick path, talking to the dog as they turned onto the sidewalk that led into town.

That left Cam with Erin, which for some reason felt awkward all of a sudden. They'd spent plenty of time together since they'd reconnected the morning Natalie had sent him to meet a prospective new tenant. He couldn't pinpoint what had changed, so he chalked the strange emotion up to fatigue and did his best to shrug it off.

"So," he began in a casual tone. "Thanks for bringing Bear to visit. Mom really seemed to like him."

"I spoke to Glenda about their program. Bear's slated for that little boy Parker mentioned, but they keep families on their waiting list. If you're interested in adopting a service dog, she'd be happy to help you work through the process. Give her a call on Monday, and she'll get you started."

Cam glanced at his mother, who was contentedly leafing through the magazine Bear had fetched for her after it fell. Obviously, he wouldn't leave her alone in the house with only a dog for assistance, but it didn't take much imagination to see that having one would make things much easier for whoever was caring for her on a daily basis.

Once she was comfortable and reasonably self-sufficient, he could get back to the life he'd put on hold in Minnesota. He missed working with the crew, not to mention the professional classes he'd been forced to withdraw from. The setback to his new career wasn't a disaster, but he'd be glad to finally get things back on track. The sooner he had his degree, the sooner he'd be designing buildings instead of constructing them.

"Did she say how long it might take?" he asked.

"No, but you could ask her." Tilting her head, she gave him a curious look. "Are you in a hurry to get back to all that snow?"

"It's not that bad, y'know," he replied with a chuckle. "The skiing's great up there."

Erin shuddered as if she could feel the chill just from him talking about it. "I'll take your word for it. See you tomorrow."

She headed toward the sidewalk, and he heard himself call out, "Erin?"

Stopping at the end of the walkway, she half turned. "Yeah?"

"Why did you ask me that? About leaving, I mean."

"No reason. Just yanking your chain."

With that, she hurried away to catch up with Parker. Cam watched the two of them strolling along with Bear, talking as they went. With the charming old homes and towering oaks stretched out on either side of the street, it was a pleasant scene that could have come straight out of a Norman Rockwell painting. While he still preferred adventure to sweetness, he couldn't deny that part of him wouldn't have minded tagging along with them.

Man, he groused silently as he dragged his tired feet up the steps, he must be more tired than he thought.

Saturday afternoon, Erin was measuring her large display windows to see how much space they'd allow for showing off the inventory that had begun to arrive. The oak floors she'd painstakingly refinished now gleamed a deep honey color, and Cam and Parker were almost finished installing the shelves and display stands they'd been building every night for the past two weeks. And Bekah had come through with a website design that was professional and easy to navigate, but fun to look at.

It was all really coming together, Erin thought with a happy sigh. If things kept moving at this pace, this time next month Pampered Paws would finally be open for business. She was envisioning how to arrange items in the windows when she noticed Cam on the sidewalk out front. He was lugging two huge covered buckets, and judging by his expression, even for him they were heavy. When he stopped to set them down, she went outside to see what was going on.

"Cleaned out the fryers this morning," he explained. "Here's your raw biodiesel."

"Great! Do you want me to hold the door while you bring them in?"

"You might wanna rethink that one. Smell this."

He took off one of the covers, and she leaned in for a whiff of the oozy mess. Jerking back, she wrinkled her nose. "Eww. Disgusting."

"Tell me about it. When I'm done playing handyman today, I'm burning these clothes."

"Careful. They might explode."

"Good point. Where do you want these things?"

Erin hadn't considered that Parker's well-intentioned project would involve tasks that probably shouldn't be done indoors. "I hate to say it, but it seems to me the farm is the best place for something gross like this."

"You want us to drive out there every time we want to work on this thing? That's nuts."

"Do you have a better idea?"

"We could do it at Mom's," he suggested in an agreeable tone that was very unlike him. The old him, anyway.

"Granddad's old workshop isn't real big, but it's got lights and electricity. And good ventilation," he added with a wry grin.

"I guess that could work. Do you think it'll be okay with your mom?"

"She'd love it. Parker's all she's been talking about since you guys stopped by yesterday. Thanks again for that, by the way. It meant a lot to her."

What about you? Erin nearly asked before she thought better of it. She and Cam had been cautiously edging closer to each other these past few weeks, and she wasn't quite certain where the line between them was anymore. He'd made it clear he still planned to leave town as soon as he could, but his commitment to stick around until the science fair made her wonder if there might be something else going on behind those dark eyes of his.

Of course, the only way to know for sure was to ask him, and there was no way she'd be doing that. Her phone chimed, and she checked the caller ID. "Excuse me, Cam. This is Parker's social worker."

Trusting him to understand her brusque farewell, she went back inside and answered the call. "Hello, Alice. What can I do for you today?"

"I have news, but I'm not sure you're going to like it."

Bless the woman for getting straight to the point. "Okay, go ahead."

"Lynn Smith wants to see Parker before she makes her final decision about you continuing as his foster parent."

"Not a chance," Erin said reflexively. "I've been trying to keep him from finding out where she is and why. He's too young for all this heavyweight drama."

"Technically, you can't keep him from her.

She hasn't rescinded her maternal rights, and she's completely within the law to make this request."

"Even though she's at least partially responsible for him being abused?"

"Even though. I'm sorry," Alice added sympathetically, "but you don't really have a choice in this. The guards are used to handling situations like this, and I can promise you they'll take good care of him while he's with her."

Since there seemed to be no options, Erin relented. "Fine. When?"

"As soon as you can arrange to get him there. If you want, you can stay in the outer lobby during their visit, but you won't be allowed inside."

"I'll definitely be waiting for him. I'll call up there and arrange a time that won't conflict with school." Recognizing that this patient, caring woman's hands were tied, Erin summoned a cheerful tone. "Thanks so much for all your help, Alice. I know you're doing your best."

"I only wish I could do more. Parker's a special little boy, and he deserves the home you're making for him. I'll say an extra prayer for both of you tonight."

"I'd appreciate that. I'll take all the help I

can get." She hung up and realized that Cam had slipped into the store when she wasn't looking. Seeing his grim expression, she joked, "Did you get all that?"

"Enough," he growled, crossing his arms in obvious displeasure. "I'm guessing you don't get a vote."

The frustration she'd been keeping down for too long burst free of her control. "Why should I? All I've done is taken in a foster child no one wanted and given him a family who love him more than anything."

"Mother's rights are tough to overturn."

That didn't sound like something he'd come up with on his own, and she stared at him in astonishment. "Where did you hear that?"

"I've been doing some research online, hoping to find something that might give you an edge."

"And?"

Grimacing, he shook his head. "She can keep him in foster care until she's released, or she can give up her claim and allow him to be adopted. It's her call."

In Erin's estimation, the worst thing in the world was feeling powerless to change a bad situation. She'd never been the helpless, wring-your-hands type, and she wasn't about to start now. "Well, if she goes that way, I'll convince her to approve me fostering him until she's out of prison. At least that way he'll have a fighting chance at a good life, no matter what happens after that."

"Are you sure?" Cam asked, scowling in obvious concern. "That sounds like a good way to have your heart broken a few years from now."

"That may be, but all his life, people have been letting Parker down. I've got no intention of being one of them."

Cam's ominous look mellowed into a slowly dawning smile. "You're amazing, y'know that?"

Admiration glittered in his eyes, sparking a flutter inside her that she hadn't felt in so long, it took her a moment to recognize it. Ever since she'd become Parker's guardian, the lion's share of her emotional energy had gone to the boy who relied so heavily on her. But now, gazing up at this stubborn man who'd gone out of his way so many times for her, she felt something else tugging at her heart.

It was Cam.

Jaded and cautious, for some reason he'd let her close enough to glimpse a side of him that she'd never even suspected was hiding under all that arrogance. Generous, caring, devoted to the few people he treasured even more than his precious independence. Instinctively, she knew that was how he'd treat his own family someday. Whoever was fortunate enough to capture his heart would never doubt that he loved her and their children with everything he had.

That was how her parents had been, and it was the kind of love Erin had always longed for but had never managed to find. Was it possible that all this time, she'd simply been searching in the wrong place?

"So…" He broke their connection brusquely, taking a healthy step back as if he'd sensed where her daydreaming was headed. "Let me know when you and Parker are going to see Lynn, and I'll clear my schedule so I can tag along."

"You really don't have to do that. It's my second visit there, so I know the drill. I'm sure we'll be fine."

"I know," he said, giving her a gentle smile. "But I'm still going."

And, with a kiss on her cheek, he strolled out the door.

Chapter Eight

Man, was he out of shape.

It was Sunday morning, and Cam had made the foolish mistake of joining Drew for a long-overdue run. The lanky farmer worked outside all week hauling hay, mucking stalls and wrangling horses. Then, on the weekends, he took tourists and campers out to the woods for hiking and some moderately exciting rafting on the creek that ran along the edge of the Gallimore Stables property. Because of that, their excursion this morning had been more of an extended jog punctuated by sections of walking that had lasted far longer than Cam would have preferred. While he appreciated his old buddy dialing back the pace so he wouldn't kill himself, he wasn't thrilled at being forced to concede that it was necessary.

Unlike February in Minnesota, the weather

was sunny and mild, and when he stopped on the front porch to stretch his tired muscles, he heard familiar voices coming through the screen door. Going inside, he was surprised to find Erin and Parker in the foyer chatting with his mother. They were dressed a lot better than he was, and he said, "You all look great. What's the occasion?"

"Isn't it wonderful, Cam?" Mom asked cheerfully. "Erin and Parker are taking me to church."

"When we were here the other day, she mentioned that she sees us walking over every Sunday," Erin jumped in to explain. "She asked if we'd stop to pick her up, and of course we said yes."

"Of course." Judging by her overly bright tone, Cam figured she knew exactly how he felt about the whole thing, and he dug deep for something else to say. "That's nice of you."

"Isn't it?" Mom chimed in, adding an affectionate look for their guests. "Parker's going to tell me all about his science project on the way."

"Do you want to come with us, Cam?" Parker asked innocently.

If the kid hadn't been so transparent by nature, Cam would've wondered if Erin had put him up to offering the invitation. Because it was Parker, Cam silenced his usual skepticism and did his best to appear casual. "Not today, bud. Thanks for the offer, though."

"Oh. Okay."

The boy's obvious disappointment made him feel like a jerk, and he found himself rethinking his answer. What harm could it do? he reasoned. He'd go sit for an hour, pretend to listen to the sermon and then leave. Nothing would change for him, but it would make Parker happy, not to mention his mother.

"On second thought, if you can wait a few minutes," he said, "I'll get cleaned up and go along."

Parker's face lit up in a delighted grin. "Cool!"

"Very," Erin agreed, adding her own smile of approval.

But it was his mother's reaction that hit him the hardest. As he passed by her on his way upstairs, she reached out and caught his hand in a weak grip. When he turned, she beamed up at him with grateful tears shining in her eyes. "Thank you, Cameron. This means so much to me."

He felt himself choking up a little, too. Not trusting his voice, he smiled back and gently patted her shoulder before continuing up the steps. As promised, he was back in five minutes, freshly scrubbed and wearing a button-down shirt and slacks. Accustomed to work boots, his dress shoes felt snug on his feet, but he figured that was a small price to pay to see the proud expression on Mom's face.

"You look so handsome," she gushed. "Doesn't he, Erin?"

Giving him a quick once-over, Erin announced, "I guess he'll do. Are we ready?"

Once they were outside on the sidewalk, Parker insisted on taking command of the wheelchair. The sidewalks were fairly level, and his passenger was light enough, so Cam agreed to let him try it.

He and Erin took up the rear, and he leaned in to murmur, "You guess I'll do? What's up with that?"

"I'm sure women tell you all the time how good-looking you are," she pointed out in a sassy tone.

"Well, yeah, but I wouldn't mind hearing it from you." She stared at him in disbelief, and he realized he'd taken a dangerous step outside the friend zone they'd agreed to maintain. "Y'know, someone who doesn't have an agenda."

"Let me get this straight. You're convinced that the women you date compliment you because they want something from you?"

"Pretty much."

"That's sad."

"Tell me about it," he grumbled.

"No, I mean it's sad that you actually believe that. What kind of people have you been hanging out with up north, anyway?"

The wrong kind, apparently. While he hadn't come back to Oaks Crossing by choice, Cam had to admit that returning to his hometown hadn't been all bad. Reconnecting with the small, close-knit community he'd grown up in had shown him another way to live. He still wasn't crazy about folks knowing his personal business five seconds after he did, but instead of resenting it the way he used to, now he understood it was because they cared about his family and the tough time they'd been having.

Far from the anonymity he enjoyed in Minnesota, that sense of belonging had its high points. Like neighbors who offered to bring a wheelchair-bound woman to church for no reason other than the fact that it was a nice thing to do.

Thinking of nice gestures prompted him to ask, "Did you set up a meeting with Lynn yet?"

"Wednesday. Parker has a half day of school, so we can pick him up and drive out there."

"What'd he say when you told him about it?"

"He was quiet, but he said he understood why we're going. I'm not sure he really does."

"He trusts you," Cam assured her. "He knows you wouldn't put him through this if you didn't have to."

"I hope you're right, but I still think he's too young to deal with heavy stuff like this. I wish I could do it for him."

The misery in her voice plucked a rare emotional chord for him. "I can relate to that. I've spent so much time the past few months taking care of Mom, I lost sight of how important it is for her to start doing things for herself again. It kills me to say it, but my dad was right."

To his surprise, Erin wrapped her hands around his arm for a warm squeeze. "Good for you."

She started to slide her hands free. On a crazy impulse, he settled his hand over them and kept them where they were. Erin looked up at him, and in those beautiful hazel eyes he saw something he never could have anticipated in his wildest dreams.

Understanding.

Women had looked at him in many different ways: affection, longing, anger. But this was the first time he'd found one who not only listened to what he was feeling but seemed to have a grasp of what it meant to him. Even more amazing, she'd praised him for it.

Erin Kinley, he mused with a grin. Who'd

have guessed that after all these years, she'd end up being the woman who got him?

When they arrived at the simple white chapel where he'd once spent so many Sunday mornings, Cam gripped the handles in front of Parker's hands to help him muscle the wheelchair up the ramp. At the top, they paused for a quick fist bump that made his mother laugh.

"Boys are always boys," she commented in a tone laced with fondness, "no matter how old they get."

The entryway was pretty crowded, and Cam pulled rank out of concern for everyone's toes. "I'll take it from here, bud. Thanks for the help."

"No problem," Parker replied, grinning up at him.

"Oh, no," Erin muttered with a grin of her own, "he's starting to sound like you."

"There are worse things," Cam retorted as they headed into the sanctuary.

"Name one."

He knew she was yanking his chain, so he made a show of trying to come up with something. Pretending to search the air for an answer, he had the distinct misfortune of meeting a pair of familiar eyes in the congregation. "My father's here."

"That's not—really?"

Cam nodded toward the pew where Dad was sitting. Alone, he noticed with more satisfaction than was appropriate considering the fact that he was in church and should have been more charitable than that.

Apparently, Mom had noticed him, too, and she said, "We should go sit with your father."

"Why?" popped out of Cam's mouth before he could stop it. She flung a chiding look over her shoulder, and he gave in to her wishes with a resigned sigh. "Okay."

"Cam?" He glanced down to find Parker gazing up at him. "Could I meet your dad?"

Erin's unconcerned expression told him that she didn't have any objections, so he tried to sound cool about it. "Sure. Come on over and I'll introduce you."

It was all very stiff and awkward, but out of respect for his mother, Cam gutted his way through it. Thankfully, Parker was oblivious to the tension between the adults and offered up some kid-inspired small talk about Bear that made the whole thing go better than it might have otherwise.

"That's incredible, Parker." Dad's approval seemed genuine, and he gave Cam a thoughtful look. "Not to mention, a worthwhile idea for someone else I know."

That they'd come up with the same way to

help Mom was surprising enough. That they were standing within arm's length and not scowling at each other was something else again. "I've been thinking the same thing."

"I'll leave the details to you, then. If I can do anything to move the process along, please let me know."

Humility wasn't a trait he recalled his father having, and Cam had to acknowledge that he was impressed. The David Stewart he grew up with had been overbearing and very much in charge of any situation that presented itself, in or outside the family. He hadn't been the warm, gracious type, but Cam had loved him because the man was the only father he had. But the cool, distant manner was all but gone now, and if they'd just met for the first time this morning, he could almost imagine them becoming friends.

The organist sat down and began playing softly to warm up the old pipes. It was everyone's cue to end their conversations and find a seat, and Cam expected Erin to herd Parker toward the section where the rest of the Kinley clan was sitting.

He was more than a little shocked when Parker asked him, "Is it okay if we sit with you and your parents?"

"Uh…" Silently consulting Erin, he got a

smile and a nod that did something funky to his gut. Whether she was agreeing to make Parker happy or because she preferred being with him, he didn't much care. After their warm exchange earlier, he was just glad she wasn't leaving him to deal with all this on his own. "Sure. That's fine."

"I'll take over from here," Dad said, smiling as he grabbed the wheelchair handles.

Since there wasn't much for him to do other than go along, Cam motioned Erin and Parker into the pew, then settled in beside them. His father parked the chair in the aisle before sliding into the end seat. He opened a hymnal and held it in front of Mom so she could see the music. Leaning toward her, he said something that made her smile, and Cam wasn't sure what to make of the whole thing.

Wasn't that the dream of every kid from a broken home? Cam mused while he leafed through the hymnal to the right page. Mom and Dad back together again. Too bad that, for Natalie and him, this little reunion was coming too late to make a difference.

Or was it?

A small voice in the back of his mind chimed in with an alternate view of recent events, and he firmly shut it down before it had a chance to become a nuisance. His family was in pieces, and had been for years. There was no fixing it now.

"Are you all right?" Erin whispered, frowning at him. "That was a pretty big sigh."

"No problem."

She clucked her tongue at him. "You really should stick with the truth. You're a terrible liar."

"You sound like my ex-wife."

"You're hopeless," she hissed, but the humor sparkling in her eyes let him know she wasn't serious about that. Funny, but now that he thought about it, Erin was one of the few people he knew who'd never let him get by with anything. Maybe that was why she'd always driven him nuts.

Resigned to sitting through a lot of off-key singing and a boring sermon, he plastered a polite look on his face and tried to give the appearance of someone paying close attention to what was happening at the front of the chapel. After greeting them all, a tall, slender man dressed in a gray suit strolled to the head of the center aisle and winged a smile around the packed seats. Cam had never met Pastor Wheaton, and he was impressed by the unconventional beginning of the service. Maybe this wouldn't be so bad, after all.

"Before I begin, I'd like to welcome back

someone who's been absent from our gatherings for far too long. Bridget Stewart, it's a blessing to see you again."

Cam had expected a hushed murmur, maybe a few smiles aimed her way. He was stunned when the congregation broke into loud applause, with a few approving whistles thrown in from somewhere behind him. Glancing back, he discovered it was the Kinley boys, and a frowning Maggie was shaking her head in dismay. Beside her, Drew grinned and shrugged at him. And even though he was supposed to be behaving himself, Cam couldn't help grinning back.

Once everyone settled down, Pastor Wheaton remained where he was, apparently collecting his thoughts. There were some papers spread out on the antique oak lectern, and Cam wondered what the preacher was up to. It wasn't often you got surprised by what went on in church, and he was curious to see where this was going.

With another smile, the pastor put his hands in his pockets and rocked back on the heels of his black shoes. "I know some of you think I just wing it on Sundays, but that's far from the truth. With God's help, I spend a lot of time preparing my sermons, and I usually think they're pretty good. But every once in a while, something happens that convinces me I need to change my tactics."

Strolling along the front of the pews, he looked like a guy out for a leisurely walk instead of at work. His casual, down-to-earth manner was nothing like the preachers Cam had detested when he was growing up, and he found himself leaning in to hear what the soft-spoken man would say next.

"That happens to all of us at one time or another," he continued in the same conversational tone, deftly including himself in the lesson. "We put together goals and make lists of what we need to do to achieve them. We work and study hard in an effort to have a good life. And then—" He smacked his hands together loudly, making the people closest to him jump in their seats.

"Something comes along to derail all our carefully laid plans with an accident, or an illness or some plain old misfortune. These things knock us off our stride, and they have the potential to destroy a family. Oddly enough, they also have the potential to bring a family closer together. Because during those difficult times, if we keep our heads up and our eyes on the Lord, we discover the great strength He has to offer His children. As all good fathers do, He will lead us out of the darkness we find ourselves in, if only we'll let Him."

After that, Cam vaguely heard the mellow drawl but not what it was saying. It was as if a pastor who'd never met him had found him in the crowded chapel and delivered the kind of encouragement he'd been needing for months. And to his amazement, some of the bitterness he'd carried around for years began to lift from his shoulders. It was as if the faith he'd turned his back on so long ago had started rustling inside him, hunting for a way back to the surface.

If it hadn't been for Erin and Parker agreeing to escort his mother today, Cam knew he'd never have voluntarily come to this service and heard those inspiring words. Not for the first time, it struck him just how much his life had changed since their unexpected reunion outside the Oaks Café. She'd been in his face—and on his mind—pretty much constantly, but at some point over the past several weeks, their encounters had evolved from barely civil to being the favorite part of his day. In fact, he realized suddenly, when he and Parker were working on the store or the biodiesel project, he looked forward to seeing her.

Not long ago, he would've brushed away his increasing fascination with Erin in favor of keeping his independence fully intact. But now, he found himself wondering if, as the pastor had suggested, God had been guiding him in her direction all along.

Chapter Nine

"What on earth is going on in there?" Erin demanded for what even she knew was at least the tenth time. Wheeling to look at Cam, lounging casually in his chair leafing through a parenting magazine, she snarled, "How can you be so calm?"

"No choice," he responded in the measured, logical tone she detested when it was directed at her. The fact that he was right wasn't what bothered her, it was that his view of the situation was far more adult than hers.

"Since when did you get to be so patient?"

His gaze lifted to hers, and he frowned. "Since I came back here to take care of a woman who was completely independent just a few months ago."

He carried all that responsibility so well, she sometimes forgot he'd given up everything to help his family. Better than any lecture, his levelheaded demeanor pierced through her angry haze. She'd blown off most of her steam pacing, and she dropped into the chair beside him, letting out a sigh of surrender. "I'm sorry for snapping at you. I'm just worried about Parker being with her all this time. I know the guards are there, but what could she be saying to him that's taking so long?"

"She hasn't seen him in almost a year," Cam pointed out. "Maybe she wants to hear what he's been doing."

Something in his tone got Erin's attention, and she turned to face him. "Is that how it is when you and your dad get together?"

"He just about talked my ear off yesterday after church. He's interested in *everything*," Cam complained, but after a moment or two, his disapproving look mellowed into the half grin she'd come to appreciate as part of his personality. "But Mom likes having him pop into town once in a while, and he's in love with his granddaughter, so it's not all bad."

"What about you?" she pressed, grateful for the distraction from counting the seconds as they ticked by on the institutional wall clock.

"It's weird to be in touch with him after writing him off when I was a teenager." He paused, as if he was deciding whether or not he should keep going. When she nodded for him to continue, she was stunned by what she heard next. "Believe it or not, you've made it easier for me to get my head around the whole thing."

"Me? How?"

Those dark eyes met hers with a look that was equal parts confused and grateful. "By listening to me rant, helping me work through this mess. After that sermon the other day, I realized that half the reason I couldn't get past what he'd done was I kept trying to pretend it didn't matter. After a while, I convinced myself that I could handle whatever life threw at me on my own and I didn't need anyone. Including God," he added in a rare show of humility.

His confession sparked a hopeful feeling inside her, not only for him but for the possibility that what had been building between them might be real enough to encourage him to stay. Their time together on Sunday had brought out emotions that she'd been trying to ignore, but every time he looked at her, they bubbled a little closer to the surface. In all honesty, she didn't know what she was going to do if he held to his original plan and returned to Minnesota. Not long ago, she couldn't wait to be rid of him. Now, she knew she'd miss him terribly.

Unwilling to give away what was going through her head, she covered her reaction with a thoughtful nod. "And now?"

"I'm rethinking that one." Reaching over, he took one of her hands and held it loosely in his. "I guess if someone was determined to keep interfering in my life, it wouldn't be so bad if it was you."

"Stop it, now," she teased, fanning herself with her other hand. "You'll turn my head."

"I'm serious, Erin," he insisted somberly. "I know it's crazy, but I think we should give it a shot."

The last of her misgivings evaporated before he was even finished speaking. Still, she didn't want him thinking she'd turned into a pushover. She knew perfectly well what he was getting at, but the girly part of her wanted to hear him say the words. Putting on her best clueless look, she asked, "Give what a shot?"

"You're gonna make me say it, aren't you?"

"Absolutely. Face it, Cam. You're divorced, and I don't have the best track record when it comes to men. What makes you believe for one second that we could make a relationship work?"

Cradling her cheek in his calloused palm,

he leaned in and brushed a gentle kiss over her lips. He hadn't said anything more, but to Erin the intimate gesture felt like a question. Beyond that, she was pretty sure it made her heart skip a couple of beats. Anything coherent she might have said went straight out of her head, and she blinked in astonishment. "Umm…okay."

A slow grin drifted across his rugged features, and he lightly kissed her again. "Good answer."

The sound of efficient footsteps coming down the hall ended their very interesting encounter, and Erin pulled away from him in an effort to regain her usual composure. She had the distinct feeling that her face was the color of a magenta peony, but there wasn't much she could do about that.

When a guard appeared in the doorway with Parker beside her, Erin offered up a silent prayer of thanks. Striving to appear calm, she stood and in a casual tone she said, "Hey there. How was your visit?"

"Fine. Can we go now?"

The terse response took her back to those first awful weeks with him, when he barely spoke a handful of words at a time and refused to look her in the eyes. A quick escape suited her, too, so she quickly signed the visitors' log and handed him his jacket. After he pulled it on, he did something he'd never done before.

Without comment, he slipped his hand inside hers and gazed up at her with the most solemn look she'd ever seen on a child. His chin trembled a bit, and she knew he was making an attempt to be brave. Instinctively, she put her arm around him and hugged him close as Cam opened the door for them to leave. If they never had to come back to this awful place again, that would suit her just fine.

Parker climbed into the middle of the bench seat of Cam's truck, staring blankly out the windshield while they settled in on either side of him. Cam looked over at her as if waiting for instructions, and she simply said, "Let's go."

After about twenty minutes, Parker finally broke the silence with a sigh so deep, Erin felt it in her bones. "My mother's a criminal."

Erin saw no point in refuting his assessment, but she searched for a way to take some of the edge off. "That's true, but she made a decision to break the law, and now she's paying for it. None of that has anything to do with you."

To her surprise, he gazed up at Cam. "My dad left, too, just like yours. Did you ever think it was your fault?"

Cam muttered something under his breath and pulled onto the shoulder. When he swiveled to face Parker, for the first time Erin saw raw, heartfelt emotion on his face. "Yeah, I did. I thought if I'd gotten higher grades or was better at sports, maybe he would've wanted me. When I got older, I realized that the problem wasn't me, or my mother or sister. It was all him, and nothing could've kept him at home with us when he didn't want to be there."

"So it was his fault."

"That's right, because he had a choice, and he chose to leave."

"I never met my dad," Parker confided for the very first time. "I don't even know who he is."

"You don't need to," Cam said in a gentle but firm tone that carried the weight of absolute conviction. "You had lousy parents, but you're a fantastic kid, and you've got a great life now. That's what really matters."

Parker took a few moments to absorb that, and Erin held her breath waiting to see what came next. Apparently satisfied, he turned to her with a slightly more upbeat expression. "I'm kinda hungry. Can we get lunch somewhere?"

Relieved that his ordeal hadn't ruined his appetite, she smiled. "Sure, honey. You can even pick where we go."

"And it's on me," Cam added as he pulled back onto the road.

Erin didn't want to give him the impression that their romantic exchange had morphed her into one of those helpless leading ladies with stars in her eyes. "I'm more than capable of buying lunch."

"My truck, my rules."

He punctuated that with a shameless wink, and she shook her head in defeat. "Whatever."

Her phone rang, and when she saw their social worker's name, out of habit her stomach launched itself into her throat. "It's Alice."

"Tell her I said hi," Parker said innocently, punching buttons on the old-fashioned radio while Erin answered the call.

"Hello, Alice. What can I do for you?" After listening for several seconds, that fluttery stomach feeling escalated into the stratosphere. "You're kidding. Really? Of course I can be there. Thank you."

She hung up and gave Parker a quick squeeze around the shoulders. "Guess what?"

He shrugged, completely uninterested. "I don't know."

"First off, your mother was very proud to see what a fine young man you're growing into."

"That's nice."

Reminding herself to keep the life-changing legal reference simple enough for him to understand, she continued. "And she signed the paperwork we need so I can adopt you."

Parker quit fidgeting and looked up at her with joy lighting his blue eyes. "She did?"

"Yes. Isn't that awesome?" she added, borrowing one of his favorite words.

"So I don't have to go away and live with her? Ever?"

"Not ever. You'll officially be my son, just like Abby is Mike and Lily's daughter."

Erin couldn't begin to describe how she was feeling, and she could only imagine how excited Parker must be. After so many months, it was mind-boggling to think that with a few signatures, his temporary stay in Oaks Crossing would become permanent.

"You should call your mom," Cam suggested as he slowed down to take the next off-ramp. "She'll be thrilled to hear the news, and then she can tell the family."

"Actually, I'd rather tell them in person, all at once," Erin responded, angling a look at Parker. "Does that work for you?"

"Sure. Cam, do you think you could be there, too?"

"I'd love to."

Laced with emotion, the mushy response

was very unlike the reserved, coolly logical man everyone—including her—had assumed him to be. When he met her surprised look with a you-can-count-on-me grin, she had no trouble smiling back.

In that moment, they became more than three people in a truck going to lunch. What they were, exactly, she couldn't say, but it felt so right that she knew they were headed in the direction God meant for them to take.

They pulled up outside a diner that promised mouthwatering food and lots of it. While Parker was in the bathroom, Erin nudged Cam's menu down to get his attention. "You were right."

"About Lynn Smith's circumstances?"

Keeping her voice low, she replied, "Last week, the parole board upheld her original sentence. By the time she's eligible again, Parker will be in middle school."

"So she ended up doing what was best for him. Gotta admit, I wasn't sure she had it in her."

"Me, too. I know we didn't talk to her for long, but she didn't strike me as the generous type."

"Maybe the chaplain convinced her that it was the right thing to do," Cam suggested. "Whatever the reason is, I'm glad this whole thing's over for you and Parker. Now you can get on with opening your store and raising your son."

Her son.

Hearing those words out loud made Erin want to cheer. Since they were in public, she muted her reaction to a delighted smile. "That sounds good to me."

"Y'know, I've been thinking about something," Cam said as Parker slid in to join them. "And I'd like to get your opinion on it. Both of you."

"Shoot," Parker piped up, making Erin laugh.

"You sounded like Drew just now," she chided. "I'm not sure I like that."

"Maybe I should spend more time with Cam," he suggested, mischief lighting his blue eyes.

"Actually," the man in question offered, "I was thinking the same thing."

Stunned by the revelation, Erin stared at him openmouthed. "What about Minnesota? Remember that job you love, and skiing and Vegas with your bachelor buddies?"

"That was fun for a while, but it's time for a change. I've got the hang of running the restaurant again, and I can take the rest of my design classes online if I want to finish my degree. There are no ski lodges here, but I like fishing and camping, and there are plenty of spots for those."

"I could go with you," Parker chimed in, clearly delighted by the prospect of Cam sticking around. "We'd have a blast."

"What about me?" Erin protested in a mock whine. "I like outdoor stuff, too."

"Sorry, Mom. No girls allowed."

The offhand comment whizzed by so fast, she almost missed it. When she registered what he'd said, it felt as if the bustling dining room came to a halt, leaving only the three of them in motion. "Did you just call me mom?"

"Yeah. You said Alice approved all your paperwork and I was going to be your son. Is it okay to call you that now?"

Indescribable joy welled in her eyes, and Erin swallowed hard around the lump that had suddenly formed in her throat. "It's very okay. Honey, I can't tell you how much that means to me."

"You're not gonna cry, are you?" he asked, obviously not thrilled by the idea of any impending waterworks.

Blinking away tears that would only make them all uncomfortable, she forced a grin. "Of course not."

Leaning over to Cam, he whispered, "Yeah, she is."

"Girls get like that when they really care about something," his buddy told him with a wink. "Ya just gotta let 'em be who they are."

Parker took that in stride and opened his menu to look over the selections. Erin stared across the table at Cam until he lifted his gaze to meet hers with a questioning look.

She rewarded him with a grateful smile, kissing her fingertips to send the gesture his way. Grinning at her, he caught it and folded it into his fist before looking down again.

Seeing Parker and Cam side by side with their heads together over their menus, Erin finally admitted to herself what she'd been trying so hard to deny.

She'd gone and fallen in love with Cam Stewart. Every maddening, generous bit of him. And it felt absolutely wonderful.

"Whaddya think, Parker?" Cam asked, turning the schematics so the boy could see them better. "Does what we built match the picture?"

Parker studied them for a few seconds and then screwed up his face in confusion. "I'm not sure. I think this part here isn't right."

"You're the boss on this project," Cam reminded him with a grin. "If you're not satisfied, then it needs to be fixed."

"It's kinda weird for a kid to be in charge. Usually grown-ups tell us what to do."

"Well, this is your idea and your contest, not mine."

"What did you do for science fairs when you were in school?"

"Nothing," Cam admitted with a chuckle. While he unscrewed the offending piece, he went on, "I wasn't into science the way you are. I liked building things out here with my granddad."

"It's a nice workshop," Parker approved, looking around at the shelves filled with all manner of labeled boxes and cans, and the tools hanging neatly on the walls. "What did you make?"

"Birdhouses, toolboxes, stuff like that. Mom still has a silverware chest I made for a Mother's Day gift when I was about your age. She's got way fancier ones in her china hutch, but she still uses mine."

"That's 'cause she's a mom," Parker informed him confidently. "That's what moms do."

"You sound pretty sure about that."

Looking down, Parker started spinning the handle of the ratcheting wrench he was holding. The ticking noise sounded loud in the silence, and Cam waited patiently for him to gather his thoughts. When the boy lifted his head, he stopped his fidgeting and said, "I didn't have a very good mother before, but I do now. I think she learned how to be like that from Grammy."

"I think you're right," Cam agreed. "Maggie's always been one of my favorite people."

"She feels the same about you."

At the sound of Erin's voice, they both turned to find her in the open doorway, holding her phone lengthwise.

"Did you just take a picture of us?" Parker asked, clearly excited by the idea.

"Several, actually. Take a look."

She handed him the phone, and he held it so Cam could see the shots, too. Some showed them working, while the last two were of them talking. Cam had been so focused on the boy he hadn't noticed her snapping away. Looking at those photos, he saw a side of himself he'd never known existed. Wearing an open, accepting expression, he looked like a father.

For someone who'd always assumed he'd inherited his own dad's irresponsible attitude, it was a real eye-opener.

"Just don't put any of those online," he ordered while Parker gave the phone back to her. "We don't want the competition knowing ahead of time what we're up to."

"Gotcha."

"What're you doing here?" Cam asked. "I thought you were unpacking boxes of pet gew-gaws at the store."

"I was, but for Christmas, Mike and Lily gave me a certificate for some pampering at the salon, and I have an appointment for this afternoon." Pausing, she added a mischievous grin. "So does your mother."

"Seriously?" While he wasn't much for fuss-ing that way, before her health had taken its worrisome nosedive, Mom had always enjoyed it. He was thrilled to learn that she was begin-ning to regain some of her customary love of the finer things. "When did you girls decide that?"

"About an hour ago. I thought a fresh cut and color would lift her spirits. Don't worry—I'll keep the price reasonable."

"Get her whatever she wants." Fishing out his wallet, he handed over his credit card. "I don't care how much it costs."

"Well, a mani-pedi might be nice."

"Whatever she wants," Cam repeated, barely resisting the urge to reel Erin into his arms for a long, grateful kiss. Just when he thought he had her all figured out, she went and did something to remind him how remarkable she was. But since Parker was here, he settled for a warm smile. "I'm real glad you thought of it."

His heartfelt comment earned him a delighted smile in return. "We girls have to look out for each other. I don't want to wear her out, so I'll keep it simple. This time," she added, waving his card in warning on her way out the door.

Cam watched her stroll through the yard and up the porch steps into the house. When she reappeared pushing Mom's wheelchair, the sound of their mingled voices drifted through the warm afternoon air. They both laughed at something as they turned to head down Main Street, and Cam let out a long, contented sigh. "Y'know what, kid?"

"What?"

"Your mom's amazing."

Parker didn't respond, and Cam swiveled to find the boy staring at him with a smart-aleck grin on his face. "You really like her, don't you?"

"Well," he hedged, then figured there was no harm in owning up to it. If a third-grader could see what was going on, there wasn't much point in wasting his breath denying it. "Yeah, I do."

"That's cool. She likes you, too."

Cam's mind flashed back to their stolen kiss

in the prison's waiting room, and he grinned. "Don't tell her, but I kinda figured that out. Are you okay with us being together that way?"

"Sure." Parker gave him a long, critical look and set his slim jaw with the kind of determination that, until now, Cam had only witnessed in adults. "Just don't do anything to make her sad."

The boy turned back to the pile of equipment they were assembling, his stern warning echoing in Cam's ears. Pragmatic by nature as well as habit, he normally made big decisions like this by analyzing all the angles and choosing the one that made the most sense to him at the time. In his current situation, there were many reasons for going back to Minnesota and picking up the life he'd enjoyed so much. Better money, professional accomplishment and freedom were at the top of that side of the list. On the other side there was only one thing.

Family.

At some point in the past few weeks, his very practical view of the future had taken a backseat to the people he cared about and who cared about him in return. Since his wreck of a marriage had ended, he'd carefully avoided entanglements because relying on anyone but himself had been too big a risk for him to take.

Just as important, he didn't want anyone counting on him, only to be let down later on.

But now, he understood that close personal connections were a good thing. They bound him to not only his own family, but to the people of Oaks Crossing who'd welcomed him back and made him feel at home. Even if he didn't deserve it.

People like Erin.

Even though it never would've occurred to him a few months ago, he couldn't help wondering what they might build together if they could manage to quit arguing long enough to make it happen. Then again, her spunk was one of the things he admired most about her. That, and the fact that she always seemed to know when he was trying to hide something from her and never let him get away with it.

"Did you think of something funny?" Parker asked in a curious tone.

"Kinda," Cam replied with a chuckle. "Except this time, the joke's on me."

Scrunching his face in an effort to follow along, the boy finally said, "I don't get it."

"Don't worry, kid," Cam reassured him, tousling his hair in a fond gesture. "Someday you will."

Chapter Ten

"Man," Cam muttered while they made the rounds of the annual Bluegrass Junior Science Fair. "Some of these kids are smarter than me."

"Some?" Erin teased, motioning toward a tricycle that had been rigged to power a night-light.

"Okay, most of 'em," he conceded with a chuckle. "Now, the kid who built the volcano that tosses out candy, that's more my speed."

He slipped an arm around her shoulders in a casual motion that had become more common lately. He seemed comfortable doing it, and she'd needed about five minutes to feel at ease with it herself. At first she'd chalked the gesture up to his growing affection for Parker extending to her, but now she suspected that there was something else going on.

She hadn't confided her feelings to him yet,

and she'd decided that pressing him for details on what he had in mind for them was out of the question. In her experience, that was the quickest way to make a man turn tail and run as fast as he could. While he seemed content with his decision to remain in Oaks Crossing, the lingering issue of him returning to the frozen north still hung between them. It was more of a defense mechanism than anything, preventing her from getting too keyed up about the possibility of a lasting relationship with him. She figured that was the smartest way to handle things, just in case he changed his mind.

Another thing she'd learned the hard way: no matter how much you loved someone, you couldn't make them genuinely happy staying with you if deep down they wanted to be elsewhere. Since she refused to twist herself into a pretzel for anyone, she'd have to be satisfied with whatever Cam was willing to give her. The approach she'd chosen was far from perfect, but at least she could live with it.

Lost in her musings, she ran into someone dressed like a robot who grunted in surprise. He pulled up short to avoid running her over, and the jerky motion caused the elbow joints in his metal chest plate to lock in an awkward spread-eagled position.

"Here, let me give you a hand," Cam offered,

carefully freeing up the pieces so the man could move again.

"Thanks. That was a close one."

"I'm so sorry, Mr. Simms," Erin apologized as she recognized the Oaks Crossing science teacher who'd been mentoring Parker. "Are you all right?"

"Just a scratch or two, nothing major. If you're looking for Parker's booth, he's on the far wall in the middle of that huge crowd of stunned parents." Since he couldn't point, he nodded in the right direction and then headed the opposite way when someone yelled his name.

Erin was anxious to see the demonstration for herself, but out of respect for the other students' hard work she forced herself to amble along and at least pretend to admire the various entries. Aside from the ones she and Cam had already seen, there was the obligatory potato-powered light bulb, a simple water clock and several models of the solar system made of everything from foam balls to ornaments painted to resemble the planets.

When they finally reached Parker's space, she hung back so he wouldn't notice her and get nervous during the spiel he'd practiced over and over at home. Then she heard him explaining his project in a clear, confident voice, and she realized she had nothing to worry about.

"As you can see in this bucket," he continued, pointing to the clear plastic viewing spot he'd suggested mounting on the side of his display, "the oil starts out pretty dirty. It tastes good when you cook fries in it, but you shouldn't put it in your car."

The throng of adults laughed, and Cam's deep chuckle rang out above the rest. Parker zoomed in on him, then flashed Erin a quick smile before resuming his presentation. He moved on to the next station, explaining that the four small buckets contained simple filters and that each one was finer than the one before it. At the final one, he set down a small beaker and turned the spigot he and Cam had rigged to drain the fuel when it was ready for use. And then, with the flourish of a seasoned performer, he poured the homemade diesel into the lawn mower engine mounted on a board at the end of the table.

After a quick pull, it started right up and settled into a loud but steady idle. Several of the onlookers gasped in surprise, and the entire group broke into enthusiastic applause. When they were done, he added one last comment.

"I'm eight years old, and I know some of you probably think I'm too young to figure out how to do something like this. So, in case you think a grown-up did my project for me, please watch this video."

"My idea," Cam murmured in her ear, clearly pleased with his forethought. "I didn't want him to be disqualified for getting too much help."

Erin found an open space where she could see the monitor better. The recording showed a montage of every stage of his project, from concept to final product. In each scene, she saw her son growing in confidence, whether the idea he'd come up with failed or succeeded.

And right behind him was Cam. Encouraging, questioning, standing back while Parker tested his theories and tweaked them to get better results. She had no doubt that Cam could've whipped up this entire system in an afternoon, but the time stamps on the various clips showed weeks' worth of trial and error that eventually produced something beyond her wildest dreams.

In that moment, it hit her. All that time, she and Cam had been doing the same kind of thing, sometimes failing, sometimes hitting all the right notes. Stubborn as two people could be, they'd found ways to work together on the store and be there when Parker needed them. For a girl who'd never been keen on relinquishing even the slightest bit of control over her life, that kind of teamwork was a real accomplishment.

The huge gym was full of people, including her very observant family, so this was hardly the time to get all mushy about Cam and her. Hoping to appear calm and collected, she shut down her brooding and plastered a smile on her face as David and Bridget Stewart came to join them.

"Parker, that was a wonderful presentation, clear and to the point," David approved from behind his wife's wheelchair. "Some of my young executives should be taking lessons from you on how to connect with an audience and keep their attention."

"Thank you, sir." Turning to Bridget, he added, "I really appreciate you letting me use your father's workshop for my project. It worked out great."

She beamed at him as if he'd just made her day. "My daddy would love knowing someone was building things out there again."

Parker gazed hopefully up at Cam. "Maybe we can make some more things together."

"I'd really like that, bud."

They traded warm smiles, and Cam ruffled the boy's hair in a gesture only he could get by with. When Erin had tried it, Parker had ducked away. Apparently, he objected when it was her, but coming from Cam, it was cool. Shaking her head at them, she wondered if she'd ever understand boys.

"Ladies and gentlemen! May I have your attention, please?" The emcee called out from the microphone on the podium set up at the front of the gym. When things were more or less quiet, he went on, "If you'd like to find a seat, the committee has finished their judging, and we're ready to give out the awards."

That got everyone moving, and in no time the milling crowd was settled. Parker sat between Erin and Cam, hands clasped in his lap in an obvious attempt to look like he was fine. But she knew from the stiffness in his shoulders how very much he wanted to take home the top award and the savings bond that came with it.

She put an arm around him for a reassuring squeeze and gave him a smile she hoped would convey how proud she was of him, win or lose. Over his head, Cam gave her a quick wink, followed by the affectionate smile that still caught her by surprise when it was aimed her way. Something was definitely going on behind those dark eyes of his, but she didn't have time to puzzle it out right now.

The lead judge handed out several prizes,

from Most Creative to Most Unusual, and Erin kept a firm rein on her impatience so the other parents wouldn't think she was being rude. Their children had worked hard, too, she reminded herself, and they'd all earned their time in the spotlight.

Finally, there was only one award left. The head of the committee picked it up from the table and held it up for everyone to see. "This is the award for Best Overall Project, as voted by the teachers and myself. This year's award, along with a savings bond donated by the Louisville Business Association, goes to a very talented third grader from Oaks Crossing, Parker Smith."

The crowd erupted into applause, while Erin and Cam embraced him from both sides. From the rear, she heard her entire family whooping with joy, punctuated by Josh's trademark high-pitched whistle. She angled sideways to let Parker get past her and was confused when he stopped in the aisle and looked back.

"What is it, honey?"

In answer, he held out his hand to her, and with tears of pride stinging her eyes, she stood to take it. Together they walked to the front of the gym where Parker calmly accepted his award, along with a framed certificate and a very official-looking Business Association envelope. He politely shook hands with the beaming judges, thanking each one in a clear, confident voice for the honor.

"Congratulations, Parker," the emcee said, his voice echoing over the speakers. Facing the crowd again, he added, "I'm very pleased to announce that Parker and his biodiesel lawn mower engine have been nominated to represent our area at the regional junior science competition being held in Lexington this summer. After that, who knows? In a few years, we may all be using this contraption on our own lawns." Everyone laughed at that, and he added, "Thank you so much for coming this evening. Please drive safely on your way home."

People began filing out, but the group that surrounded Parker afterward was still pretty huge. To Erin's surprise, he handled the attention well. He was a far cry from the timid boy she'd met nearly a year ago, clinging to the arms of a chair in Alice's office, scared to death of everything and everyone, she thought, blinking rapidly as fresh tears threatened to break free and embarrass them both.

"All right, everyone," Maggie declared, holding her arms out wide, "victory party at the farm. Bridget, the girls and I have been cooking all afternoon, so I hope you're hungry!"

As they left the school and went into the parking lot, Cam chuckled. "You've been cooking, bug? That doesn't sound like you."

"Someone has to run to the supermarket when the chefs run low on butter and eggs," she shot back.

"Now, that I believe."

The three of them climbed into his truck and on the drive out to the farm, Parker asked, "Cam, I know you're gonna be real busy this summer, but do you think you could come to Lexington with us?"

"Is that what you want?"

Parker nodded eagerly. "More than anything."

Cam slid a questioning look Erin's way, and her heart leaped into her throat. Swallowing to make sure her voice wouldn't come out in a humiliating squeak, she said, "I thought you had big plans for the diner. You know, increase revenue so you can get a buyer to take it off your hands."

"Sometimes, little things are even more important."

"Meaning?"

"I'm not gonna sell the Oaks. I'm gonna keep it and run it myself, make sure the business stays in the family."

"You mean, for good?" Parker gasped.

"For good."

Erin couldn't believe what she was hearing. This from a man who'd fled their hometown the second he was able and had only returned for the holidays or a family emergency. "Why?"

"Come on, Mom," Parker scoffed, rolling his eyes. "He loves you. Can't you tell?"

"Whaddya you know about it?" Cam demanded with a scowl that didn't have much punch with his eyes twinkling the way they were.

"I see Mike and Drew with Lily and Bekah," he explained as if it should have been obvious. "You two look the same when you're together."

"We do?" Erin asked, stunned by his revelation. "I didn't know that."

"Well, I'm pretty smart for a kid."

"Yeah, you are," Cam agreed as he parked in the turnaround at the farm. Stepping down, he opened his door and growled, "Now, get out."

Parker scrambled from his seat and raced to the porch where Charlie and Sarge were waiting for their company to arrive. Coming around the truck, Cam opened the door for Erin and offered his hand. "Wanna take a walk?"

"Sure."

He kept her hand in his, and she had to admit she liked the feeling of all that strength being wrapped around her. When they got to the fence rail that enclosed the front paddock, he turned and took her other hand, too. He looked like he didn't know quite how to start, but she reined in her characteristic impatience and gave him time to pull his thoughts together.

Finally, he gave up and simply said, "Erin, I love you."

That fluttery feeling in her stomach blossomed into an entire flock of butterflies. "I love you, too. And I'm so glad you're staying."

"Yeah?" Reeling her into his arms, he dropped in for a long, promising kiss. Nosing along her jaw to her ear, he murmured, "How glad?"

"I guess you'll have to stick around and find out."

His low chuckle tickled her ear. "I guess I will."

Resting her cheek on his chest, she cuddled into his embrace and let out a deep, heartfelt sigh of contentment. Whatever their future together might hold, in her heart she knew that this was the start of something wonderful for them.

And she could hardly wait to see what came next.

The next morning, Cam was wrestling a section of shelves into place at Pampered Paws when his phone chimed a ring tone he hadn't heard in months. Surprised by the sound, he checked the caller ID to see his boss's number flashing on the screen. He turned down the volume on his portable stereo and answered the call.

"Hey, Jeff. What's up?"

"Look, I know you resigned and everything," his former boss replied, getting right to the point as usual, "but I've got an offer you might not be able to pass up."

Now that he'd committed to staying in Oaks Crossing, Cam wasn't all that interested in anything other than finding someone to sublet his Minneapolis apartment. Then again, Jeff Burlingham had promoted him from the crew to foreman and encouraged him to pursue the education he'd put off for so long. Cam figured the least he could do was hear the man out. "Is that right? What've you got in mind?"

"The architect for my next job just bailed on me, and I'm up against a deadline that won't budge. I'm hoping you can help me out."

"I'm not accredited for that kind of work yet," Cam reminded him. "You need a pro."

"I've got the plans. I need you to do the specs and run the project. You've been doing that for a couple years now, anyway. This would just make it official. And it pays better."

There was the kicker, Cam thought morosely. To balance the books, he'd been running the Oaks Café for a small salary that wasn't nearly enough to cover his portion of Mom's nursing care. Alex and Natalie couldn't contribute any more than they already were, and the savings he'd been tapping into were gone. He was fairly confident that Erin would end up purchasing the building from them, but even if Natalie expedited the sale and closing, the influx of cash would come too late to be of much help.

If he couldn't come up with a way to bring in more money, they'd be forced to cut back on the one thing that Cam refused to tinker with: Mom's visiting nurse. Her recovery was still maddeningly slow, but she was making steady progress every week.

"I appreciate your confidence in me, Jeff, but I'm not so sure."

"This project is scheduled to break ground in two weeks, but that's not gonna happen unless I can find someone who's qualified to step in and make it work. If you sign on, I'll bump your foreman's pay by twenty percent."

Cam quickly did the math and almost dropped his phone in shock. "You're kidding."

"I'm desperate," Jeff corrected him tersely.

"This isn't a personal favor. It's business, and I need an answer from you ASAP."

Cam had never been one for overthinking things, especially not when someone presented him with a golden opportunity like this. He'd always approached tough decisions with logic, and that approach had never steered him wrong. As great as the idea seemed on the surface, he had more than just himself to consider now.

"I'll let you know tomorrow," he finally said, just as Erin appeared at the end of the aisle with the missing shelf support he'd been hunting for. "Thanks for the offer, Jeff. I really appreciate it."

He disconnected and took the brace from Erin, whose grim expression told him she'd heard more than enough of his conversation. "I'm guessing that was your boss."

"Yeah."

"He needs you back in Minnesota?"

Cam nodded, and while he bolted the support into place, he filled her in on the rest. She didn't say much, but when he was finished, she gave him a stern look. "You're not seriously thinking about turning that down, are you?"

"Well, yeah, I was."

To his surprise, she smacked his shoulder. "Why on earth would you do that? This is what you've been working so hard for. So now you're considering throwing all that work and education away? For what?"

She was without a doubt the most aggravating woman he'd ever known. It didn't help that not long ago, he would've agreed with her line of reasoning. But now, he put aside logic and went with his heart. "For us. I love you, and Parker, too. I want us to be together."

"Don't you dare put this on me," she spat, backpedaling to get away from him. "If you want to stay for yourself, fine. But if you do this for any other reason and it doesn't work out, you'll be miserable. And you'll blame the person who kept you here when you really wanted to go."

"Kept me here?" he echoed in disdain. "You really think you've got that kinda hold on me?"

Her eyes flashed defiantly, reminding him that her fiery spirit was the thing he'd always liked most about her. "Well, isn't that what you're saying?"

Cam tried to hold on to his anger, but it was no match for this strong, determined woman who loved him enough to let him go. Sherry had left him in self-defense, but Erin was fighting him to ensure his happiness with no regard for her own. It was maddening and sweet, all at once. Just like Erin. "Yeah, I guess I am."

"All right, then."

Her stony expression softened considerably, and he slid his arms around her, drawing her close for a long, lazy kiss. Pulling back, he rested his forehead on hers with a deep sigh. "Love you, bug."

"I really wish you wouldn't call me that."

"I know."

Epilogue

"Is it always this busy?" Glenda asked Erin when they caught a breather from a steady stream of customers and phone calls on a Saturday morning.

"When we've got a new batch of kittens from the shelter playing in the front window, it is," Erin replied with a laugh. Handing her friend a bottle of cold water, she added, "Business has been great ever since we opened, but I guess you weren't counting on such a hectic pace when I hired you to work here part-time."

After a long swallow of water, Glenda smiled. "The extra money definitely comes in handy, and my kids love coming here to visit while I'm working. It's a real boost for the Canine Helpers, too. All those business cards I brought in the other day are gone, so I'll have to print up some more for you to give out."

"You can do that back in my office if you want, assuming you can find the card stock in all that mess. I really need to wade through everything and design some kind of system. Between the business and all the school events Parker's been involved with, I just can't seem to find the time."

Glenda glanced at the window in the front door with a little grin. "Why don't I take care of that for you? It looks like you've got a customer who might prefer the personal touch."

Before Erin could ask what on earth she was talking about, Glenda was already on her way toward the back of the store. When the bells over the front door jingled, Erin turned to find Cam strolling into the shop. Hectic as her morning had been, it all disappeared the moment she saw him.

Coming around the counter, he slid his arms around her and pulled her in for a long, toe-curling kiss. Drawing back, he gave her the lazy grin she'd come to adore. "Hey."

"Hey yourself." Picking up a stack of invoices from the counter, she fanned her face with them. "That was quite the greeting."

"The Oaks is in the black for the second straight month, and Dad loves the office I outfitted for him at the house, so I'm having a killer day. How 'bout you?"

"I just finished the books, and thanks to Bekah's website, Pampered Paws is this far from turning a profit." Holding her thumb and forefinger a quarter of an inch apart, she couldn't help gloating just a little. "I think it's safe to say we're a big hit."

"That's fantastic. Congratulations."

"Thanks, but there's more. I got a call from that vet Josh's friend told him about. Heather Fitzgerald."

"And?"

"She finished her residency last month, and she'll be available soon. We're going to do a video chat next week, but from what I heard today, I think she might be just the kind of person we're looking for to fill that position at the rescue center."

"Also fantastic."

She was still getting used to his understated way of celebrating, but after a moment she picked up on the excitement that he was trying so hard to mask. The gleam in his eyes alerted her that there was more he wanted to tell her. "Okay, your turn. What's got you in such a sunny mood?"

"Is Parker around?"

"Upstairs figuring out a strategy for that new video game you bought him, so he can beat you next time you guys play. Why?"

Without explaining, Cam said, "Call him down here, wouldya?"

She couldn't imagine what was going on, but she did as he asked. When the three of them were together, Cam stood opposite them and looked from her to Parker and back. After being in such a hurry, all of a sudden he was hesitating, and her instincts told her something very important was about to happen.

"I've always been the kind of guy who prefers to be on my own," he began in a straightforward manner that did absolutely nothing to ease her mind. "That way, no one ever got close enough to hurt me. Unfortunately, it also meant that no one ever got close enough to see who I really was and decide if they liked me or not."

"I like you, Cam," Parker chimed in earnestly. "I think you're the best."

Honest gratitude softened his chiseled features. "Thanks, bud. That means a lot to me."

"I guess you're okay," Erin commented, hoping to lighten the mood a bit. "I mean, we've been together every day for the past few months and haven't killed each other yet."

"Y'know, that's what I love most about you," he said with a warm smile. "You always tell it like it is."

It wasn't the most romantic thing she'd ever

heard, but then again this was Cam. He could be almost brutally direct, but she never wondered what he was thinking or if he was being straight with her. When he told her he loved her, she believed him without question. It was a huge improvement over all the time she'd wasted on dead-end relationships, trying to guess what a man was thinking. "Come to think of it, I feel the same way about you."

"I was hoping you'd say that."

Fishing around in the front pocket of his jeans, he pulled out the kind of little velvet box every girl dreamed of getting someday. To be honest, she'd almost given up on ever receiving one herself. "Is that what I think it is?"

"Let's find out." With the maddening grin that used to aggravate her beyond measure, he opened the box with a little creak. Nestled inside was a vintage diamond ring that couldn't have been more her style if she'd gone to the jeweler's and chosen it herself.

Gazing up at him in amazement, she gave him her biggest, brightest smile. "Cam, it's gorgeous."

"I'm glad you like it." Looking from her to Parker again, he said, "I love you both more than I ever thought was possible. Will you guys marry me?"

"You mean, like, be a real family?" her son stammered, eyes shining with delight.

"A real family," Cam confirmed, glancing over at Erin. "Whaddya say?"

"I say yes," Parker blurted, wrapping his arms around them both in an exuberant hug.

"What about you, bug? I know I'm not perfect, but I can promise you I'll always do my best."

The vow came straight from his big, generous heart, and it was the most wonderful gift anyone had ever given her. Erin rested her hand on his cheek and smiled up at him. "That's all I could ever need."

"Is that a yes?"

Realizing that she hadn't officially answered his question, she laughed at her own foolishness. "Yes."

Parker whooped in excitement, dancing around them while Cam slid the beautiful antique ring onto her finger. Lifting her hand to his lips, he gave her the warm, gentle smile she'd come to adore, knowing it was meant especially for her. "Thank you."

"You're welcome."

From outside, she heard cheering and a growing swell of applause. Bracing herself for what she knew she'd be seeing, she looked out to the crowd that had somehow gathered in front of the shop without her noticing. She'd been so focused on Cam and his life-altering request that she'd missed the fact that twenty or more people had clustered together on the sidewalk in front of Pampered Paws.

"What did you do?" she demanded with a laugh. "Invite half the town?"

"To possibly watch me crash and burn? Not hardly."

"Then what are they all doing here?"

Turning back, she realized that while everyone had been cheering on their engagement from their vantage point on the sidewalk, now their attention was fixed on the deep window well full of adorable kittens. Tapping the glass, children were making smooch faces while their parents traded looks that even from a distance said, "Should we?"

"Looks to me like you're gonna have some disappointed customers," Cam noted with a chuckle. "You've only got half a dozen kittens, and there's three times that many people out there."

"Not a problem," Erin assured him, picking up the cordless phone and pressing the speed dial for the Oaks Crossing Rescue Center. "Hey Sierra, it's me. We're having a run on kittens here in town. Can you send someone out with that batch of calicos we got the other day? Oh, and send Abby, too. If they tag-team these folks, I'm sure she and Parker will have them all adopted out in no time. Thanks a bunch."

Her waiting customers had apparently decided the coast was clear, and they began filing in the door, most of them making a beeline for the kitten playpen.

When she hung up, she saw Cam grinning at her, shaking his head. She had no idea what he thought was so funny, and she asked, "What?"

"You're amazing, y'know that? No matter what problem comes up, you've always got a solution." Leaning in, he gave her a quick kiss. "I've never been into smart women, but I gotta admit you're starting to grow on me."

"Is that why you're marrying me?"

"That, and you've got a great kid." As he angled his eyes toward Parker, his face took on a pensive expression. After a moment, he went on, "Something just occurred to me. Your adoption's almost done, and I know after that you were gonna change your last name. What would you think of changing it to Stewart?"

The boy gave Erin a questioning look. "Is that what you're gonna do?"

"Yes. I'm pretty traditional when it comes to things like that."

He thought that over for a few seconds and then nodded. "Parker Stewart. That sounds good."

"Yeah, it does," Cam approved, putting an arm around both of them for a cozy family hug.

Standing there with two of the handful of guys she'd ever met who disproved her "boys are stupid" theory, Erin smiled at each of them and added her opinion.

"Perfect."

* * * * *

If you loved this tale of sweet romance,
pick up these other stories
in the OAKS CROSSING series
from author Mia Ross.

HER SMALL-TOWN COWBOY
RESCUED BY THE FARMER

And check out these other stories
from author Mia Ross's previous miniseries,
BARRETT'S MILL.

BLUE RIDGE REUNION
SUGAR PLUM SEASON
FINDING HIS WAY HOME
LOVING THE COUNTRY BOY

Available now from Love Inspired!

Find more great reads at
www.LoveInspired.com.

Dear Reader,

Welcome back to Oaks Crossing!

The moment sweet, shy Parker Smith showed up at a grade school play in *Her Small-Town Cowboy*, he grabbed my attention. From his awful past to his more hopeful future, he showed so much potential I just knew I had to write a story that would give him the happy ending every foster child deserves.

Erin felt much the same way when she first met him. Lost and alone, he needed plenty of understanding, patience and love, all of which she was more than willing to give him. But as much as she cared about him, she recognized that he needed things she didn't have. Finding those things in Cam was a big surprise for her, not to mention for him. That these two old rivals could put aside their differences to focus on the present is a testament to what people can accomplish when they're determined to succeed.

While their working together began as a practical matter, gradually they began to appreciate each other in a more personal way. Both of them were inspired by Parker's bright optimism and compassion for the people and animals he met during his time in Oaks Crossing. His attitude encouraged them to take a step back and view each other with fresh eyes. This new perspective allowed them to recognize traits they'd never noticed before and take their first steps toward becoming the forever family that Parker wanted more than anything.

If you'd like to stop by for a visit, you'll find me online at www.miaross.com, Facebook, Twitter and Goodreads. While you're there, send me a message in your favorite format. I'd love to hear from you!

Mia Ross